D1579383

About the Author

Kent was raised in Taiwan and in Sweden. He has also lived in USA, Switzerland, Denmark and Belgium, before making a home in Scotland in 2014. Living in various places has taught him to integrate enthusiastically in each new environment.

The places he has lived and the people he has met have influenced his life and shaped his multifaceted personality. These experiences continue to enrich and impact his approach to challenges and appreciation of life.

Kent is private, a thinker, an explorer and enjoys cooking and feeding friends. He believes in fate and reincarnation and is bad at DIY.

LETTING GO

Kent Hung

LETTING GO

Vanguard Press

VANGUARD PAPERBACK

© Copyright 2019
Kent Hung

The right of Kent Hung to be identified as author of
this work has been asserted by him in accordance with
the Copyright, Designs and Patents Act 1988.

All Rights Reserved

No reproduction, copy or transmission of this publication
may be made without written permission.
No paragraph of this publication may be reproduced,
copied or transmitted save with the written permission of
the publisher, or in accordance with the provisions
of the Copyright Act 1956 (as amended).

Any person who commits any unauthorised act in relation
to this publication may be liable to criminal
prosecution and civil claims for damages.

A CIP catalogue record for this title is
available from the British Library.

ISBN 978 1 784656 40 9

*Vanguard Press is an imprint of
Pegasus Elliot MacKenzie Publishers Ltd.*
www.pegasuspublishers.com

First Published in 2019

**Vanguard Press
Sheraton House Castle Park
Cambridge England**

Printed & Bound in Great Britain

Dedication

This book is dedicated to those whose paths have crossed and will cross with mine, and to all the positive, negative, happy, unpleasant, loving, heartbreaking, enriching, disappointing encounters and exchanges, without which I would not have thrived and become a happy person.

Special dedication to Mrs McLain and her family.

Acknowledgements

The inspiration of the book came in the autumn of 2016 during a sleepless night with banging headache, following a housewarming party of an ex-colleague in Copenhagen, Denmark. From the development of first initiative, first character, first plot, first story line, first chapter to have finalized the manuscript in autumn 2018, it has been a challenging yet fulfilling and interesting journey.

To Abbott and Mari (and many others) — without your encouragements and honest suggestions, it's possible that the book would not have been finalized or gone in this direction.

I sincerely hope that this is a beginning of an adventure rather than an end of a project and that the characters and storylines have somewhat moved and touched you like they did for me when I created them.

Chapter 1
Their Paths Cross Again

Andrew was lying in bed. It was already past one in the morning, and even though the door to the guest bedroom was shut, it felt like the loud dance music was shaking the whole house. He almost regretted coming to Olivia's welcome party for Justin.

Justin Grey had been Olivia and Nathan's best friend when they were in the USA and had recently got an internship in Glasgow as part of his Master's programme. He'd be spending six months in Glasgow, where Olivia and her husband Adrian lived.

Andrew had first met Justin about eleven years before, when Justin was nineteen, the same age as Nathan and Olivia were back then. As Andrew lay in Olivia's guest bedroom, he couldn't help wondering what Nathan might have grown up to be like. It was great to see how Justin had developed into a vibrant and polite young man.

The music was still pumping. For a while Andrew just stared at the ceiling and wasn't able to sleep. Most of the guests had already left. Only

Olivia, Adrian and two of Olivia's work colleagues, as well as Justin, remained. They were now dancing to a twenty-five-year-old hit of Madonna, 'Vogue', but, strangely, Andrew was able to doze off, even with the loud music playing and the noise from people talking and laughing.

Andrew was half asleep when he noticed that the music had stopped. He became aware that his door was open. He thought that maybe someone had opened the door by mistake. But even in his stage of sleepiness, instinctively he felt the presence of someone in his room. As he was lying facing the wall with his back to the door, Andrew was worried that the person who had entered the room would be able to see him wearing nothing but his tiny, tight briefs. He turned around to see a face approaching him. It was Justin.

Justin, who was now sitting on the edge of the small single bed, whispered, "Mr Hughes."

"Oh, hi, Justin. How are you? Is the party over?" Now Andrew was awake and realised that the house had gone quiet. He sat up in bed. As it was a hot and humid summer night, Andrew didn't have much of the duvet covering him, exposing his partly naked body. Although approaching fifty, Andrew still had a good head of hair, kept fit and could easily have been mistaken for being in his late thirties or early forties.

Andrew wasn't able to move at all without the risk of revealing himself. At that point, although the light wasn't on, he felt flushed and more exposed than if he were actually naked. 'Where is the rest of that damn duvet?' he thought, realising he wasn't able to pull the duvet towards him because Justin was sitting on it.

"Yes, everyone's left and it's now three o'clock." Justin's voice sounded a little frightened and nervous. Andrew could smell alcohol on his breath. Suddenly, Justin leaned forward and gave Andrew a hug. With his head very close to Andrew's ear, he whispered, "Mr Hughes, I'm so happy to see you again, and I would like to tell you I often think about Nathan." Andrew thought that the hug, though brief, was sincere and heartfelt, and yet he felt shocked lying there half-naked, and just looked at Justin's boyish, innocent face without knowing what to say. A few seconds later, Justin stood up. "Good night, Mr Hughes," he said. "I am sure we will catch up in the morning, I am staying over as well." He closed the door and left the room.

Andrew was frozen in the same position for a while. He wondered what had just happened. He felt that something was going to change his life, without knowing exactly what it would be. He was then flooded with emotions and lots of memories surfaced, so much so that he struggled to go back to sleep. For

Andrew it felt a bit surreal to hear Nathan's name from someone from the past who he had met about eleven years ago. Yes, it was eleven years since Nathan had died, and it was then that he had also met Justin. Andrew thought about Nathan every day, but he almost never talked about or mentioned Nathan to other people. Although he and Olivia met up from time to time, they seldom talked about Nathan, because it was an area neither of them wanted to touch.

He woke up early next morning to find the whole house was very quiet. His lack of sleep was telling on him. He had an overwhelming headache and a slight hangover, all he wanted to do was go home to his own bed. He still felt puzzled about Justin entering his room in the middle of the night, but convinced himself that Justin had perhaps had a bit too much to drink and that the alcohol had made him a bit sentimental. Andrew thought it best not to torture himself with it.

In order to avoid waking anyone up and facing Olivia, Adrian and Justin, he did his best to get dressed quickly and leave quietly. In order not to worry Olivia, he left a note and put it on the dining table, telling her that he was taking an early train back to Edinburgh and promising to call her later that evening.

As soon as he opened the door and got outside of the house in the fresh air, he felt much better. It was early Sunday morning and the shops were not yet open, the streets were still very quiet. Andrew took the subway to reach Queen's Street station, where he got on the next train back to Edinburgh. He slept for most of the journey back.

Arriving home, he debated whether to take a shower first before going to bed, but he was too tired and exhausted. He jumped into bed and fell into a deep sleep.

At the same moment, Olivia woke up. She stretched her arms and saw Adrian next to her, still in a deep slumber. She had a slight hangover and was dying for a cup of coffee. She got hold of her mobile and took a look at it, but had to concentrate to see what time it was; just before ten a.m. She hid herself under the duvet, hoping to continue to sleep.

'Coffee, coffee. I need coffee.' Her craving for caffeine won her over. She contemplated for a few seconds, then made an effort and stood up. She had to hold on to the side table in order not to trip over. She put on her dressing gown and glasses and slowly walked downstairs. Her body was aching. She looked around the living room. 'Not bad,' she thought. Her guests had helped her to clear up and had put most of the dishes and wine glasses in the dishwasher.

She picked up a few bowls and yawned as she walked quietly towards the kitchen. She shut the kitchen door with a push using her bum, then opened the bin and emptied the leftover party snacks from the bowls before putting them in the dishwasher. She turned on the tap, holding the kettle underneath to fill. As she was waiting for the water to boil, her mind went into a form of trance.

'How surreal is it having Justin and Andrew in my house at the same time? one sleeping in the guest room next to the living room and one on the sofa-bed in Adrian's office. It must have been more than ten years since I last saw Justin, when I was released from the hospital before coming back to Glasgow.'

Her mind wandered further and it dawned on her that the piece of the puzzle that connected them was Nathan. 'Gosh, I haven't thought about Nathan for a while.'

She made herself a cup of coffee and took a sip, though it was boiling hot. She took a deep breath and felt calmer. A piece of paper was lying on the kitchen table. She picked it up and realised from the note that Andrew had already left.

"Good morning." Justin opened the door and yawned.

"Oh gosh. You scared me." As her mind was still not totally awake, Justin's appearance had taken her by surprise. She took a look at him, his clothes all wrinkled and hair messed up. He must have fallen asleep still fully dressed.

"Good morning. Were you able to sleep at all? Do you want some coffee?"

"Thanks." Justin nodded his head twice and yawned again.

"Andrew already left."

"Really? Why? Is he okay?"

They walked through to the guest room next to the living room. They opened the door and, sure enough, there was no sign of Andrew.

Olivia saw that Andrew had already stripped off the bed linens and, neatly folded, had placed them on the bed. 'Typical Andrew,' she smiled. "Yep, he left a note and said he went home early," she said.

Olivia walked back to the kitchen. Justin followed. "Something wrong? Is he angry about something?" Justin asked tensely.

"Why should he be angry?" Olivia made a cup of coffee and handed it to Justin. She looked at Justin, puzzled by his question.

"I…" Justin almost wanted to tell Olivia that he had walked in to Andrew's room last night. Olivia looked at Justin without saying a word as a sign, waiting for him to continue.

"I… I just thought maybe he was angry that we played music so loudly so late and he wasn't able to sleep. I was looking forward to catching up with him.

17

The last time I saw him was when I helped to clear up Nathan's room before he went back to Scotland... Blimey, it feels like a lifetime ago."

"I don't think he is angry about anything. I guess he just wanted to go back to his own bed." Olivia yawned again. "Do you want me to make you some breakfast?"

"No, thanks. I'm not hungry. I will head back to my place soon. I still have to unpack my luggage and get ready for my classes starting next week."

"I'm going back to bed." Olivia came over and gave Justin a hug.

"Do you think he would mind if I sent him a friend request on Facebook?"

"Oh, I thought you were already friends with him. Why would he mind?" Olivia did not understand why Justin made such a big deal of it. She walked upstairs with the cup in her hand, but stopped halfway, turned and asked Justin, "Is everything okay?"

"Yes, everything is okay. Thanks for the party. I'm going to leave soon."

"It was a great party. Hey, don't be a stranger. Come any time you want. Just shut the front door when you leave."

Justin went back to Adrian's office and sat down on the sofa-bed. He turned on his computer and found his Facebook page. He searched and found Andrew.

He stared at his computer, contemplating for a while, and finally pressed the 'Add Friend' button as if he had just made a life or death decision.

At the same moment, Andrew was awoken by his mobile phone.

There were a few text messages from Olivia, asking why he had left without saying goodbye, and a voice message from his childhood friend, Jimi, who lived in Spain. Andrew also noticed a friend request on Facebook. Andrew clicked to see who had sent the request — it was from Justin. Andrew put down the phone, sat up in bed and thought about whether he should accept or not.

Would it be impolite and a bit odd to reject this request? He pondered only for a few brief seconds and then clicked 'Accept'.

While he was still thinking about it, a Messenger message came from Justin.

Good morning, Mr Hughes. Great seeing you last night after so many years. Glad to see you doing well. I will be visiting Edinburgh Uni for a meeting in two weeks. Would be great to catch up again if you have time. Justin

Still half asleep, and without thinking, Andrew instantly replied.

Yes, it was great seeing you, too. If you come to Edinburgh and need a place to stay you are welcome to stay over at my place. I have a guest room and would be happy to show you around Edinburgh. Andrew. PS call me Andrew.

Andrew got up and went for a shower. As he was getting dressed, another message arrived, again from Justin.

Thanks, Mr Hughes. I look forward to catching up. I have been dreaming about Nathan lately. Meeting is scheduled for a Friday, so I will come down on Thursday evening. I will txt you to confirm the arrival time before I purchase my bus tickets. Thanks again. Justin.

Andrew went to the kitchen and made a cup of coffee. He had an urge to tell Jimi about Justin, but then stopped himself, as he didn't know what he would say. After Justin entered his room last night, Andrew was now curious to find out more about what had happened in Justin's life since the last time they had met in Upstate New York eleven years ago, and to hear about his studies and his fiancée Rebecca, who Justin had mentioned the night before at the party. Though he felt excited about Justin's visit, Andrew still wondered exactly what was beneath his desire to see Justin again. He then argued with himself. 'Why should I need to justify? I don't need a reason at all.'

Andrew texted Jimi just briefly, reporting on the party at Olivia's and how he had sneaked home that morning, self-conscious that he had omitted to mention anything about Justin. They exchanged a few more texts. Jimi invited Andrew to visit him and Vincent in Spain, and Andrew told Jimi that he would check his calendar the next day to suggest a few possible dates.

As Andrew put down his phone, he entered a curious state of mind. 'Oh gosh, it was eleven years ago! Who would have thought then, when I first met Olivia, that one day in the future she and I would become good friends?' Olivia was Nathan's girlfriend and was in the car accident and was with Nathan when he died. It was even more unimaginable and even more of a surprise for Andrew to see Justin again, who he had first met at Nathan's wake.

As he sat thinking, the names of the people he knew, or had known, associated with Nathan popped into his head; his mother, Lena, Jimi, Mama Evelyn, Olivia, Justin and many more who had been and were still in his life. He took a trip down memory lane, to his childhood.

Chapter 2
Growing Up
Part I

Andrew didn't know his father, Neil Hughes. Neil had left for New Zealand when Andrew was an infant. His mum Hilary didn't talk about or mention him much, so Andrew didn't ask much either.

Apart from photos taken on the day of their wedding, his mother only kept a handful of photos of Andrew's dad. Two were of the three of them together, one was of his dad and mum together and two were of his dad alone.

Growing up, Andrew had looked at those photos often, though he hadn't given them much consideration and had forgotten about them after his mother had put them away.

Many years later, when he was clearing out his mother's flat after her passing, he found those photos again, hidden inside a shoebox in one of her cupboards. He took a closer look at them and discovered that his father was not looking directly at the camera lens in any of the photos. It seemed strange to Andrew, as if he had wanted to be disconnected somehow.

Andrew's father, Neil, had a brother, Uncle Steve, but they were never close and the two of them had apparently fallen out over their inheritance when their mum died.

When Steve and Neil were little, their father bought a corner shop in Stockbridge, which the Hughes family ran even after their father had passed away and the two boys were in their early teens. Then, when the boys' mother died a few years later, she left the corner shop to Neil, causing a further feud between the two brothers.

Andrew was told by his mother once that although Uncle Steve was the eldest, he was irresponsible and reckless when it came to money. Occasionally, he was late settling bills with suppliers and a few times money disappeared from the till after Uncle Steve had been minding the shop.

So, even before Neil left them, Hilary didn't have much contact with her husband's side of the family. Andrew didn't even remember meeting Uncle Steve. Andrew's first childhood memories were of his mum and his mum's twin sister, Aunt Betty.

Andrew's mum and Aunt Betty were adopted when they were little girls. In their adopted family, the girls had a very strict and religious upbringing and didn't have fond memories of their childhood. As a result, they didn't keep in contact with their adoptive family once they had grown up, and Andrew had no recollection of the family.

The reason why Hilary and Betty deliberately avoided having contact with their adoptive family once they moved out was to do with a traumatic childhood experience, which both girls kept secret between them.

When Hilary was about fourteen, at home alone, she answered the door to a vacuum cleaner salesman. After discovering there was no one else home, he had forced himself on her and raped her. When Betty and the girls' adoptive mother came home from food shopping, they found Hilary lying on the kitchen floor, traumatised by the assault.

Discovering what had just happened, Hilary's adoptive mother ignored her distressed and vulnerable state and shouted hysterically at Hilary, blaming her for the rape. "You shouldn't have opened the door. You must have said something to lead him on. You have brought it on yourself and you are to blame."

Both Hilary and Betty were utterly shocked and uncomprehending of the abusive words and accusations their adopted mother threw at Hilary. From that moment on, they lost any respect and all trust in her. That event and those feelings of betrayal scarred Hilary and Betty unimaginably for life.

"Your body is now dirtied and stained, and no one will ever want to marry you," the adoptive mother had said. The incident was not reported to the police, and that was the end of the matter. She warned the sisters not to discuss it. The secret was never to come out.

Looking at her poor sister, Betty felt hopeless, as she wasn't able to protect and stand up for her, nor could she defend her from this appalling and unfair verbal attack. As if what had physically happened to Hilary that afternoon wasn't cruel enough.

When Hilary's adoptive father came home from work, they acted as if nothing had happened. Everything was as usual, dinner on the table, their adoptive father asking about their day in school and the girls clearing the dishes and doing the washing-up.

That evening, Hilary and Betty held each other and sobbed, and swore this would be their secret. No one would ever know. They also vowed to each other to "leave this place" as soon as they were financially able.

From that moment on, it had cluttered Hilary's mind, and the experience had left her feeling unclean. Although she knew it wasn't her fault, those cruel and harsh words spoken by her adoptive mother at the time caused permanent wounds to her psyche. Hilary became quite rigid and distant, shunning any affection or hugs.

Little did she know that when she became a mother, her behaviour and wounded personality would have a profound effect on her son, Andrew. Little Andrew was already a quiet and sensitive boy. In life, both he and his mother Hilary were not comfortable receiving and showing affection, vulnerability and emotions towards others and even towards each other.

It was no surprise that both Hilary and Betty followed through on their promise and left their adopted home as soon as they were old enough and were able to support themselves financially. Hilary didn't go out much and had never had a boyfriend. Betty was the outgoing one, as she had always been. One evening, she dragged Hilary out to a local pub for a drink with a few friends to celebrate Betty's job promotion. It was during that evening that Hilary met Neil. He was twenty-four and she was twenty-two at that time. They got talking and later, although there wasn't much of a spark between them, they started seeing each other.

Neither of them liked hanging out in bars, wasting money on alcohol, so, apart from going to the movies from time to time, they often met in Neil's flat. Hilary would cook them meals using ingredients Neil had collected from the corner shop that had just passed expiry date and could no longer be sold. At times, they also invited Betty and her boyfriend, who later became her husband, to join them for dinner.

One evening, a few months after they had first met, Hilary told him she was pregnant. Neil looked down at his shoes and mumbled a proposal. "Should we get married, then?" As if it was the most proper and natural thing in the world.

They didn't have a large wedding, neither having nor wanting to spend too much money on it. They just closed the corner shop for a few hours and went to a registry office during the day with two witnesses; one was Betty and one a friend of Neil's. In the evening, Hilary and Betty prepared a meal for the four of them to celebrate the occasion. They did push the boat out a little with a bottle of bubbly that Neil had got from a supplier for free.

It was so simple and fast, they didn't even go on a honeymoon, partly because they didn't have the money. They were saving up for the baby. But it was enough for Hilary. It was Hilary's dream to start her own family. Furthermore, as she was adopted, this was a way of mending her wounded past. She longed so much to have a place where she belonged and where she thought she could start her life all over again like a blank sheet of paper.

Hilary worked as a nurse when she first met Neil, but decided to quit her job after they got married so she could help her husband with the corner shop. She

27

moved from the flat she shared with Betty into Neil's tiny two-bedroom flat in the Stockbridge area, only a few minutes' walk from the corner shop. Betty also moved in with them for a while, before she got a smaller place of her own right after Andrew was born.

Neil was thrilled when the baby arrived. He was a kind person, a good father. He was hard working and responsible. He didn't drink heavily and was never abusive. The bills were always paid on time and Hilary and Andrew were cared for. But Neil was a quiet soul, he didn't reveal much of himself.

Hilary knew their marriage wasn't based on love, but she thought having a family of her own and now with Andrew and a business to run, though it was just a corner shop, was enough for her. She thought it was enough for Neil, too. She imagined their lives would just plod along.

So, when Andrew was just over a year old, it was an utter shock to her when Neil told her he wanted to leave for a while to go to New Zealand to stay with a mate from school who had emigrated there and had a sheep farm where Neil could work.

For the first few months, Neil sent money home and a handful of postcards to Hilary, but then contact ceased.

"Haven't you tried to contact him or write to him?" Andrew remembered asking his mum once, when he was about seven.

"Yes, I wrote a few letters, but I heard nothing back from him. Then the last letter I sent was returned unopened and his name and address crossed out. It was marked on the front of the envelope that the recipient no longer lived there."

That was the last time Hilary spoke about it, and it was the last time Andrew asked about his father.

Because Neil left Andrew and Hilary when Andrew was little, for a long period of time while growing up Andrew felt strongly that it was his fault that his father had left them.

As Andrew grew older, he often wondered how his mother had agreed to his father's departure and to a place so far away. He had imagined many times in his head what kind of conversations and discussions they might have had before his father left, the circumstances that caused his father to leave and the reason his father had not kept in contact or wanted to return.

He thought that it must have been heart-breaking for his mother to accept her fate and agree with his father's wishes to leave, only to realise that he wasn't going to return. 'How did she manage to handle all the legal and official burdens that went with his disappearance?' With those questions embedded in his head, he regretted terribly that he hadn't had the courage to ask more questions about his father and discuss it with his mother before she died.

Hilary, though a loving and caring mother, had been on her own for many years, so she was used to making rational and practical decisions rather than emotional ones. As a single mother, it had not always been easy for Hilary, and at times she wished she had been more lenient in bringing up Andrew. But decisions had to be made, bills had to be paid and food needed to be put on the table.

Although they weren't poor, raising a child on her own meant that Hilary was always careful with her money. Aunt Betty and her husband used to bring Hilary and Andrew food and take them out for dinner now and again. One Christmas, Aunt Betty spoiled Andrew, buying him the largest chocolate Santa available. Andrew was beside himself with joy and excitement. Hilary would only have given him practical gifts.

Aunt Betty and her husband and children visited often, before she and her family emigrated to Canada. Andrew had fond memories of the family and of playing with his younger cousins.

Hilary was devastated when Aunt Betty told her when Andrew was about five that the family was moving to Canada. After they had left, it took Hilary a while to get used to their absence. Aunt Betty was more than just a sister to her, they were twins and had taken care of each other for years. After they moved, they only came back for one visit.

Hilary kept in close contact with her sister in the beginning with letters and short phone calls during the holiday season and birthdays. Then, before her grandson, Nathan, went to the USA, he taught Hilary how to use a computer so that she was able to talk more often with her sister using Skype allowing them to see each other via computer screen.

Aunt Betty's family moving to Canada was another devastating disappointment that little Andrew couldn't understand. He always asked himself, 'Why do all the people I love leave me? Have I done something wrong? Am I not worthy to be loved?'

From early on in his life, as a defence mechanism, he learned to detach from his feelings and people so as not to get hurt again when people inevitably left. He struggled constantly with an unrecognised and unresolved separation anxiety. Andrew often did his schoolwork in the corner shop after school so his mother could watch over him. He was a handsome, quiet boy, but did not like it when people came too close to him or showed him affection. Customers used to squeeze and pinch his cheeks and mess up his hair, and he hated it.

Aside from Andrew's emotional trauma, his life with his mother at the corner shop proved uneventful and for the most part peaceful, but that was all to change...

Chapter 3
Growing Up
Part II

About two years after Aunt Betty and her family moved to Canada, an Asian lady — Evelyn Wang — entered Hilary's shop. She and her husband had immigrated to Edinburgh from Hong Kong with their two children, Joey (Joseph) and Jimi (James) just over a year before. Their daughter, Sami (Samantha) was born in Edinburgh a few years later.

Evelyn Wang and her husband, Edmond Wang, opened a Chinese takeaway a few doors along from Hilary's shop.

At first, they remained polite and friendly, but after a few months, Evelyn and Hilary had got to know each other very well and they talked to each other often. Evelyn became a regular visitor to the store and also brought Joey and Jimi with her a few times. It didn't take long before the two women became good friends, bonding the two families and their fates in various ways.

Hilary learned that Evelyn actually came from an affluent family. She and her older brother were brought up by a nanny and tended by servants, a driver and a chef. Her father, Dr Lin, was a well-known medical doctor in Hong Kong. Her grandfather, father and later her brother were all medical doctors.

Even before she came of age there were matchmakers knocking at the door with potential suitable husbands, all from wealthy and respectable families. Evelyn attended several organised dating events, but got bored after the first few. Evelyn didn't like any of the proposed suitors, though her parents had their eye on a suitable young man whose family owned a large import/export business of traditional Chinese medicines.

The problem was, Evelyn had a secret. Evelyn was in love. She had fallen in love with the family chef's son, Edmond — a tall and handsome young man who grew up with Dr Lin's family after his mother started working for them. At a young age, Edmond had started working as a kitchen helper and intern in a Hong Kong-style restaurant, and only visited his mother from time to time when he was off work.

No one had suspected that these two young hearts were falling in love. One day, someone spotted them in a park walking hand in hand and informed Evelyn's father, Dr Lin, and that's when the war started. Evelyn was told never to see Edmond again and was locked in her room for days. Edmond's mother was sacked and forced to leave Dr Lin's home, where she had worked and lived for over fifteen years.

Evelyn was furious. With help from a servant she managed to escape from her room and went to live with Edmond and his mother. After she eloped, to save face and the reputation of the family, Dr Lin put an announcement in the newspaper that Evelyn had no more connections with the Lin family. Evelyn vowed never to see her family again, now that they had disowned her.

For the first few years of their marriage, Evelyn and Edmond both worked in restaurants, he as a sous chef and she as a kitchen helper and chopper. They worked very hard to make ends meet. Then, Evelyn became pregnant and had a baby boy, Joey, followed by another son, Jimi, three years later. Even though this small family didn't have much money, they were happy.

"At first I didn't even know how to boil hot water, let alone work in a kitchen or do any housework or take care of newborn babies," Evelyn chuckled. "I was very grateful to have Edmond's mother living with us, as she helped with the boys. She taught me many things. She was good to us. Then she became ill, so I took care of her for a few years before she died. Joey was devastated, as he was practically brought up by his grandmother. Jimi was too young to remember or to know what was going on." Evelyn became tearful.

"Here," Hilary whispered, and handed Evelyn some paper tissues.

Evelyn took time to dry her tears and recollect her thoughts before she continued. "That was the happiest time in my life. We worked very hard and were self-sufficient. My husband became a Hong Kong-style kitchen head chef and I helped in the kitchen making a few simple dishes. We didn't have much money, so he used to bring me flowers left over from wedding banquets he had prepared food for, and this warmed my heart for days." Evelyn blushed like a teenager when she described it to Hilary, and they both giggled.

"When Joey was about seven, one year after my mother-in-law died, my husband started gambling and didn't even come home some nights. People started coming to the restaurant demanding his debts be settled. It got so bad it came to the point where he lost his job and wasn't able to land another job, as his reputation spread among restaurants. I was devastated, not only was Edmond gambling, he also started drinking and seeing other women." Evelyn became emotional again. "At one point, my husband went into hiding and was nowhere to be found."

Evelyn sighed. The debtor had sent two guys to pay Evelyn a visit, she explained.

"Mrs Wang. Sorry to disturb you. Where is your husband?" They had said it politely.

"No idea. I am also looking for him."

"I am not sure you are telling the truth. The money owed has to be settled no matter what." The two guys were still polite, but Evelyn knew they meant business.

"I don't have money, and I am also looking for my husband." Evelyn felt hopeless and frustrated with Edmond.

The two guys looked around and their eyes laid on Joey and Jimi. They smiled. "Mrs Wang, if your husband doesn't show his face and the debt is not paid, we will have to keep something as bail."

"What are you talking about?" Evelyn held the boys tightly next to her.

"We will be reasonable with you. We will give you five days. If the debt is not settled then, we will come back. We will be nice and reasonable, we will only take one boy. It will be your choice, which one do you prefer? Remember, five days and we will be back. Don't even think about going to the police or running away." The two guys laughed as they left. Evelyn fell down on the floor and Joey and Jimi were crying, even at their young age they knew something wasn't right.

Fearing for her children's safety, it was a very hard decision, as it stripped her of all her pride, but, left with no other alternatives, she contacted her mother through a cousin, who arranged for them to meet without her father knowing.

"You see, I didn't have a choice. We got threatening messages from men sent by the debtor. If we didn't pay, they would kidnap Joey and Jimi." Evelyn still showed fear in her eyes when she told the story to Hilary.

When Evelyn finally met up with her mother, her mother cried her eyes out. She was thrilled to meet Joey and Jimi, but felt so bad seeing her own daughter in such a desperate state. In tears and shame, Evelyn knelt down and bowed in front of her mother, asking for forgiveness for the pain she had caused her and the family. She told her mother that she couldn't face her father and asked whether her mother could help her.

Without any hesitation, Mrs Lin paid off all of Edmond's gambling debts. He must have heard the news from talk on the street, as a few days after the debts were settled and paid off, Edmond reappeared and returned home.

Mrs Lin later visited Evelyn and Edmond. Edmond kept his head down all the time and couldn't look Mrs Lin in the eye, while he swore to her and Evelyn that he would never gamble again.

Later, in order for Edmond to get away from a bad crowd and from the temptation of gambling, Mrs Lin also managed, through a long-distance relative, to get Edmond to move to Edinburgh to work as head chef in a Cantonese-style Chinese restaurant there.

Evelyn saw her mother a few more times while they were waiting for their visas before coming to Edinburgh. However, her father eventually found out and put a stop to her mother seeing them. Actually, Evelyn was his favourite, and she later learned from her brother that her father kept whispering her name, looking at her photos in tears on his deathbed — but, as his foolish pride got in the way, he had forbidden Evelyn to be contacted before and after he passed away.

Ding. Ding. The bell above the door rang. A customer pushed open the door and entered the shop in the middle of Evelyn telling Hilary her story. Hilary and Evelyn stopped talking abruptly and looked almost guilty — like kids being caught eating too many sweets.

Hilary greeted and took care of the customer while Evelyn was talking quietly and playing with Andrew. *Ding. Ding.* The bell rang again as the customer pushed to exit and the door closed.

"And what happened next?" Andrew asked eagerly, as soon as the customer had left. Both Evelyn and Hilary burst into laughter, as they hadn't noticed

Andrew paying attention to the story. Evelyn gave Andrew a hug, and from that moment on the two held a special bond.

"Anyway, we came to Edinburgh, and both of us worked in a Chinese restaurant for almost a year," Evelyn said. "Then we heard about a Chinese takeaway becoming vacant and we bought it. Luckily, we had some savings and some additional money that my mother had given me."

Hilary and Andrew were invited to have dinner with the Wang family a few times. Andrew became good friends with Jimi as they were the same age, but he was most fascinated by Edmond Wang. As Andrew had never had a father-figure, he was longing to have a male influence in his life.

When Andrew first met Edmond, he looked up to him, thinking that he was the coolest guy he knew. Edmond smoked heavily and swore both in English and Cantonese when takeaway orders became too hectic.

Edmond was a handsome, tall Asian man with thick, dark hair. He liked to make jokes. He thought it was funny to teach the boys to say dirty swear words in Cantonese and then ask them to repeat them, which in turn reduced him to tears of laughter.

While Jimi did everything possible to avoid getting involved or helping in the restaurant, Andrew loved hanging out in the Chinese takeaway after school, because he liked spending time in the kitchen with Edmond. Edmond was always friendly towards Andrew, and when Andrew was a bit older, he was allowed to help out, bagging takeaway containers ready for delivery. Andrew also used to go along with the delivery guys distributing takeaway orders to customers' homes. As customers would tip them extra when Andrew handed over the bags, the delivery guys made a deal with him, he could come along on deliveries whenever he liked and they would share the tips with him.

About three years after the Wang family had arrived in Edinburgh, their daughter Sami was born. Edmond was overjoyed to have a daughter.

"Can you believe it? He changes Sami's nappies, which he never did with Joey and Jimi!" Evelyn would tell Hilary with a mixture of disbelief and fascination.

Sami was her father's pride and joy. She was the closest to him of the three children and also the most affected by her parents' divorce. After Edmond passed away, following many years of illness, Sami never got over her father's death.

When Sami was about a year old, Evelyn told Hilary that she had found out that her husband's gambling and womanising habits had started up again.

When they first arrived in Edinburgh, Edmond had been surprisingly committed and responsible. However, as the takeaway business started doing well and he got to know some local Chinese restaurant owners and workers, the gambling and drinking resurfaced. At one point he stopped working at the takeaway restaurant and didn't show up or come home for days. As history repeated itself, Evelyn was visited a few times by men unfamiliar to her, demanding that she settle her husband's gambling debts.

"I thought moving to Edinburgh would give the family a chance to start afresh and that my husband would change. How foolish I was, disobeying my own parents." Evelyn's thoughts were far, far away. "I deeply regret that I didn't see my mother and my father ever again. My mother died only a few months after I came to Edinburgh and my father a few years later. At times, I still dream about my mother's teary eyes and my father's disapproving look staring at me."

When Sami was about two, Edmond and Evelyn finally got divorced. Edmond moved away from the Wang family to live in another part of Edinburgh. Evelyn told Hilary that she had to borrow large sums of money to buy her share of the takeaway from her ex-husband.

Edmond was a talented chef, so finding a job wasn't difficult. He got plenty of offers, and from what Evelyn heard, he even had a few female companions, but he never remarried or really settled in to his new life. He wasn't good at living by himself and he missed seeing the kids, especially Sami.

Evelyn raised their three children alone. She was a father, a mother and a provider for her family. Although their father did not die until Joey, Sami and Jimi were adults, Edmond was an absent father in every sense of the word. "Maybe I owe him something from a past life," she would say philosophically, and sigh. She told Hilary that more than once she had to bail her ex-husband out financially, even after their divorce.

Many years later, Edmond developed Alzheimer's disease and spent his final years in a care home. Evelyn and Sami visited him regularly, and the whole family was with him during his final days.

Evelyn told Hilary that at the funeral she had burnt a few decks of cards, some fake US dollar notes and even some adult magazines — a Chinese tradition — to send those things over to the other side for the deceased to enjoy. "At least now he can lose as much as he wants without me worrying about his gambling debts." Evelyn's words sounded detached, though she was visibly sad about her ex-husband's passing. Edmond was the first and only man she ever loved.

Evelyn had been an important figure not only in Hilary's but also in Andrew's and even Nathan's lives. She helped Hilary to raise Andrew, and later Nathan. Evelyn insisted that Andrew call her 'Mama Evelyn'. She was like another aunt to him and an extra grandmother to Nathan. She adored Nathan and was more affectionate towards him than her own grandchildren. One of her regrets was that Joey's boys were not close to her. For some reason or because of some misunderstanding between them, Joey's wife never liked Mama Evelyn, so she wasn't invited to take much part in her grandchildren's upbringing and lives.

The only time Mama Evelyn got angry with Andrew was when he and Jimi were about thirteen. A chef told Hilary that Jimi and Andrew had hidden in the storage room in Mama Evelyn's takeaway restaurant, trying out cigarettes. She yelled furiously at them and made the two youngsters know how disappointed she was with them both. Jimi and Andrew were furious, too, and confused, as the chef was the one who had given them the cigarettes and encouraged them to smoke in the storage room. They found out later that it was a prank, the chef had done it on purpose, as he thought it was funny to get them into trouble.

Jimi told Andrew later that his mother wouldn't look at him or speak to him for a week. Mama Evelyn made a promise to Andrew not to tell Hilary, and Andrew never touched cigarettes again, but he knew Jimi was a social smoker at parties — of course without Mama Evelyn knowing.

Hilary and Evelyn trusted and safeguarded each other and their children, and the two supported each other through thick and thin. They went to the same church and they both played bridge at the same club every Thursday evening. They loved to watch their favourite TV programme, *The Long-Lost Family*, and wept together. Andrew knew that deep down his mum would wish to find her biological parents.

Occasionally, Andrew also watched the show and talked to Jimi about it. More than once, Jimi encouraged Andrew to contact the show, asking for help to find Neil, Andrew's father. Andrew was tempted, and even called the show to find out more details, but never went through with it. He was afraid of what he might find out, and also he didn't want to upset Hilary, as he wasn't sure how she would have felt about it because she never spoke or mentioned much about Neil to Andrew. Andrew knew the subject of Neil was sensitive and off limits with his mum, so he didn't want to bring it up.

Andrew didn't remember when or how the two women got the idea, but his mother and Mama

Evelyn encouraged each other to deposit £20 a month into a special account. Hilary put the account in Andrew's name. She showed Andrew the bank statement and told him several times in a detached voice, "This will help you to bury me." Andrew looked at her with a blank face as a form of silent protest, because he didn't find it amusing.

Andrew and Hilary tasted the food from the takeaway restaurant many times, but a different world opened up to Andrew the first time Mama Evelyn prepared an authentic Chinese meal and invited him and his mother over for dinner. She also introduced Andrew to Chinese opera and her favourite Chinese dish — chicken feet prepared with black bean sauce. Andrew loved it, Jimi absolutely hated it. He preferred British home cooking.

Mama Evelyn also introduced Feng Shui principles to Andrew, which he later integrated into his interior design business, making him stand out from his peers. "Today is not a good day for you to sign the contract... Today you will meet someone influential if you head north." These warnings from Mama Evelyn put a smile on Andrew's face whenever he thought about them. Although Mama Evelyn was a churchgoer, in addition she was a strong believer in Feng Shui and a great follower of the Chinese moon calendar, which she studied rigidly for recommendations before making any important decisions.

Her knowledge of Asian cuisine cultivated in Andrew a very sensitive taste for truly authentic Asian food. Andrew learned a lot about Asian cuisine, not only from Mama Evelyn but also from the chefs who worked for her through the years. More than once he also brought some of the dishes he prepared to Mama Evelyn's restaurants and received high praise from her and the chefs. His specialities were drunken chicken and beef in satay sauce with chilli. Andrew was so interested in Asian cuisine that he even wrote and published many articles on Asian food and recipes as a food critic.

At one point, when Andrew was so focused on his writing, no one wanted to go out for dinner with him, especially Nathan, who thought Andrew was such a pain because he was always making excessive notes and passing comments about every detail of the food, the menu, the decor and service of the restaurant. Nathan and Sami, however, remained Andrew's best audience and guinea pigs. Both happily ate everything he cooked when he was experimenting with new recipes at home.

When Andrew first met Joey and Jimi, Joey was ten and Jimi was seven, the same age as Andrew. Joey didn't want to play or spend time with them as he was older. Joey had his own circle of friends. But the two boys, Jimi and Andrew, became good friends. They used to have sleepovers at each other's homes, and they both loved taking care of Sami. Sami was their shadow and followed them wherever they went. As Sami was ten years their junior, Andrew and Jimi treated and spoiled her like a little princess, especially after Evelyn and Edmond's divorce.

Jimi and Andrew were the same age, but since he was born in January and Andrew in June, Jimi never let Andrew forget that he was actually one year older according to the Chinese moon calendar. They went to the same school and were in the same class. They supported each other when either of them was teased or bullied. Jimi was very popular at school. He quickly mastered the English language, albeit with a heavy Scottish accent. He spoke better English than anyone Andrew knew. Even at a very young age, Jimi had a way of talking to the girls. Jimi was a social butterfly, and Andrew became his 'plus one'. They sat next to each other in class all the way through to National 5. Although they both passed the National 5 exam, Andrew didn't continue with Highers and Advanced Highers, like Jimi did.

Jimi was accepted at Edinburgh University to major in International Relations. Jimi continued with his studies and embarked on a Master's, eventually getting a scholarship to Geneva University in Switzerland. After doing well in an internship programme with one of the United Nations agencies, he was offered a permanent position working for the UN in Geneva, Switzerland.

Andrew remembered one of the sleepovers he and Jimi had had when they were about ten, the two of them were lying in bed and talked about what they wanted to do in the future when they grew up. Jimi had said, "I want to travel the world." He did just that — both for work and pleasure.

"I don't want to move too far away from my mum. I just want to grow up and have a family and have children," Andrew had said. Andrew never moved away from Edinburgh.

At nineteen, baby Nathan came into Andrew's life.

Chapter 4
Nathan

When Andrew told Hilary that he had got a girl pregnant, she was not as furious as Andrew had feared. Hilary was more surprised than angry. She did ask, though, whether they were going to get married before the child was born and about Andrew's plans to go ahead with his university studies. Somehow, she was secretly excited about becoming a grandmother, though she didn't think of herself as quite that old. She also didn't consider herself to be a good mother to Andrew. Due to the circumstances that had shaped her life and because of her personality, even though she was a loving mother, she wasn't an affectionate mother to him. In her mind she now had a second chance to raise a child.

At the time most people, including Andrew and maybe even Jimi, had thought that if anyone was to get a girl pregnant before marriage it would have been Jimi, which was probably Mama Evelyn's biggest worry.

Mama Evelyn was over-excited and couldn't hide her enthusiasm (or maybe she was just happy it wasn't Jimi). She often told Andrew that she'd remain "Mama Evelyn" even to the baby, as she felt she was too young to be called anything else. She told Andrew and Hilary that she would take good care of the pregnant girl and provide her with some Chinese herbal medicines and remedies and special dishes — all supposed to be good for women before and after giving birth.

When Andrew finally found the courage to tell Jimi that the girl they had met at the party was pregnant with his child, Jimi thought Andrew was pulling his leg. "It was all your fault," Andrew jokingly blamed Jimi, as he was the one who had dragged him to the party and got him drunk.

Andrew was so drunk that night that he threw up a number of times. He didn't have much recollection of the evening, but he remembered Jimi going to a room with a girl, so Andrew had done the same. He thought this was the norm and what was expected of him. It had taken Jimi quite a while to remember who this girl was.

On hearing the news, Jimi looked long and hard at Andrew, finally asking, "How do you know it's yours?"

Andrew was stunned by the question. For the first time in his life, Andrew felt that he wanted to punch Jimi, but after a moment of reflection he realised that maybe the question was not so strange

51

after all, and one that many people would probably ask. Andrew felt he needed to make it clear to Jimi, and anyone else, that there was never any doubt in his mind, he knew it was his child. "Jimi Wang, you are such a twat! Of course, I know it's mine. Unlike you, we were both inexperienced when we met. Find it funny if you want. I couldn't care less."

"No, I'm not laughing. I'm sorry for what I said." Jimi put his arms around Andrew and gave him a hug. "I am here for you. Tell me what happened!"

Andrew told how he got quite a surprise when the shy foreign girl he'd met at the party came looking for him in the convenience store a few months after they had first met. She must have gone to a great deal of trouble to find him. He couldn't remember if he had told her where he lived or if he had mentioned the whereabouts of the store. She told him that she had been there a few times before, but only saw Hilary minding the store, so she had left.

The girl was relieved when she saw Andrew, but she also seemed very worried, nervous and unsettled at the same time. She asked to speak to him in private. Hilary was out shopping with Mama Evelyn, so only he and Sami were there. Sami liked to hang around the store. Although she was only eight at the time, she was more than capable of taking care of and dealing with customers. Andrew asked Sami to look after the store for a few minutes, but told her to call him if customers came in.

He took the girl to the storage room in the back, where she hesitated and struggled with her words at first, but finally told him, "I am pregnant with your child."

Andrew was shocked and dumbfounded. He stood there looking at her for a long time without being able to speak. After the initial shock, Andrew was able to talk to the girl, asking her about her pregnancy and how she was doing.

"I want to keep the child." The girl said it nervously to Andrew, and her whole body was shaking, as if she was afraid of him thinking of something else.

The girl was Lena, Lena Wallin, a Swede who had come to Scotland to work as an au pair. She met Andrew that night she got pregnant with Nathan. A few months into her pregnancy, she quit her job as an au pair and moved in with Andrew and Hilary. It was a difficult time, all three had to learn to live together under the same roof, as well as figure out the changes in their lives.

Lena was a lovely and polite young girl who got along well with Hilary. But Hilary soon sensed that these two youngsters were not "a couple", as there was no suggestion about the two getting married. But she admired them both for wanting to go ahead with the pregnancy.

Lena went back to Sweden to visit her family and came back to Edinburgh three months before the baby was due. It was agreed that her parents should come to Edinburgh a few weeks before the birth.

One evening, two months before the due date, Lena felt a sharp pain in her belly and was rushed to hospital. The doctor told Andrew and Hilary that they would try to prevent a premature birth for as long as possible. It was a long wait, but early next morning the doctor decided it wasn't possible to wait any longer and injected Lena with a shot of Pitocin to induce labour. Later that evening, Mama Evelyn, Jimi and Sami also came to the hospital to keep Andrew and Hilary company.

At 3.19 a.m. on 3 January 1987, Jonathan (Nathan) Aaron Hughes was born. Both Andrew and Lena were to turn nineteen later that same year.

Lena came home after a few days without Nathan. He was premature and had to stay in a neonatal intensive care unit for a few weeks. Right after she gave birth, Lena developed crippling postpartum depression and didn't want to visit Nathan in the hospital. She spent most of her days crying and staring out of the bedroom window.

Andrew and Hilary visited Nathan in the hospital as often as they were allowed, and several times a day they even took along Lena's breast milk; the intensive care unit also fed Nathan with a special milk formula, as Lena wasn't able to produce enough milk. At first, the baby wasn't feeding. He was tiny and fragile and his weight gain was worryingly slow, to the point the doctor was alarmed. Then, after a few days, his intake of Lena's breast milk and milk formula normalised and after a few weeks Nathan was able to come home.

Sadly, Lena didn't know how to bond with her baby. She didn't know what to do with Nathan or how to adapt to her new role. Her parents rushed to Edinburgh just a few days after Nathan was born, but after a few weeks' stay they returned to Sweden. At that time, Lena felt extremely lonely and homesick and wasn't able to cope with her new life as a mother.

Mama Evelyn and Sami came almost daily to visit Nathan and brought with them bags of Chinese takeaways. "You must eat." Mama Evelyn would open the takeaway containers, showing Lena what she had prepared. "These dishes are made especially for you to give you strength after giving birth."

Luckily, Lena loved Chinese food and ate everything Mama Evelyn prepared, most of them off-menu. Her taste buds changed and she began to crave spicy food and would get through a large tray of Kung Pao chicken in five minutes flat.

Due to lack of sleep with baby Nathan constantly crying, Lena's mental well-being fluctuated. Lena's moods were infectious, and Andrew wasn't that happy either, especially when he hadn't had any sleep. They weren't in a relationship and no one was to blame, but it broke Hilary's heart to see Lena so miserable. She supported Lena as much as she could, while still allowing Andrew to take charge. She was also worried when she realised that Andrew was also clueless and found his new role as a father and the new circumstances scary and overwhelming. "How foolish I am to think otherwise? Andrew is still just a child himself," she told Evelyn.

One morning, when Lena was preparing milk formula for Nathan, she forgot to check the temperature and didn't close the bottle tightly enough, accidentally spilling the hot liquid over him. Nathan was rushed to hospital with minor burns and the case was investigated by child social services. It was a demanding and stressful period for all of them.

Lena spoke to her parents and after several long discussions they agreed that it would be best if she went back to Sweden alone without Nathan; at least for a short period of time to begin with. Nathan would stay behind to be cared for by Andrew and Hilary.

Chapter 5
Starting from Zero

Around the time of Nathan's birth and Lena's return to Sweden, there were many challenges and changes confronting the Hughes family.

The corner shop wasn't doing as well as it used to. On the same street there were a few newly opened chain convenience stores that Hilary couldn't compete with. Hilary wasn't prepared to invest the prohibitive sum of money needed for new technologies or to buy the rights to become a franchisee; so, with encouragement from Evelyn, she sold the corner shop.

Meanwhile, Evelyn's takeaway business was really booming and she wanted to expand, so she asked Hilary if she'd be in charge of the fish and chips section of the business in order to attract even more customers.

After Nathan was born, Andrew didn't know what to do with his life or what kind of job he'd be interested in or suitable for. He didn't embark on his university studies and didn't have any plans for his immediate future.

It just so happened that Joey had recently moved to Newcastle and opened a Chinese restaurant there. Jimi was busy with his new life at university and was talking about moving to London for his studies. Sami was too young to help out in Mama Evelyn's takeaway, and so Andrew worked on a part-time basis for Mama Evelyn while taking care of Nathan. Andrew knew this wasn't his destiny, but what was it to be, then?

Mama Evelyn had a vision of expanding her business further and wanted to sell the takeaway to buy a proper restaurant. She sought Andrew's help to search for her dream restaurant. Andrew contacted a few agents that dealt with buying and selling commercial properties and after several meetings he found one particular owner of a small agency that he got on well with. Mr Douglas Walker had been working in the business for most of his life and was looking forward to retirement in a few years.

Mr Walker showed Andrew and Evelyn a few potential restaurants and finally she decided on a place located in the centre of Edinburgh. In appreciation for his hard work in finding the restaurant for her, Evelyn Wang also engaged Mr Walker to sell her takeaway business.

The restaurant needed a lot of renovation and none of them had any experience in doing this type of work, so Evelyn asked Andrew to see if Mr Walker could recommend the right tradesmen. They knew Mr Walker had been in the property business for many years and had some very good contacts. Andrew made an appointment to see Mr Walker in his office.

Looking at Andrew very seriously, Mr Walker asked, "So, Andrew, what are your plans for the future?"

"I'm not sure yet. I have a little boy, Nathan, who is only one, so my priority is to take care of him. I am helping Mrs Wang with the restaurant, and after that I might go back to university," Andrew answered, knowing there was a hint of uncertainty in his voice.

"Look, young man. You seem to be a decent, polite and intelligent guy who is not afraid of hard work; what about if you came to work for me? I'll teach you what I know and in a few years' time I can sell the business on to you. My children aren't interested in the estate agent business, so I don't have anyone to leave it to." Mr Walker spoke as if it were the most logical, natural and reasonable thing one should do.

"Listen, Mr Walker, thanks for the offer and your faith in me. I'll discuss it with my mother." At first, Andrew was speechless and taken aback by the offer, but suddenly he felt there was a light at the end of the tunnel and that he might be able to make something of himself, despite not having continued with his studies.

"Yes, talk to your mother. It's going to be lots of hard work, but if you are not afraid of hard work and you do it right, you'll be rewarded," said Mr Walker, with a smile on his face. He shook Andrew's hand as he left. When Andrew got home, he discussed it with Hilary and they both agreed that it was a great opportunity; mainly because they didn't know what else Andrew was going to do.

Andrew started working for Mr Walker, who was a fair but strict boss. Since he knew nothing about this kind of business, Mr Walker made sure that Andrew learned everything from scratch, and, at times, the hard way. Mr Walker said to Andrew repeatedly that the best way to learn was from your own mistakes.

Mr Walker really saw Andrew as his successor. Since none of his children wanted to take over the business, he trained and taught Andrew all the insider tricks of dealing with tradesmen, solicitors, banks, mortgage lenders and insurance agencies. While he was working for Mr Walker, Andrew was often invited to Mr Walker's home for dinner and social gatherings; he got to know the family well. More than once, Mr Walker jokingly said to Andrew that he would have been a good candidate for a son-in-law. Andrew just laughed it off.

They renovated and refurbished Evelyn's new restaurant, even exceeding her expectations, which wasn't easy. Evelyn was not an easy customer to please, as Mr Walker quickly realised. But Mr Walker was a smart businessman and he knew that if he delivered and completed this job well, on time and within budget, he would receive more business from Evelyn's connections in the Asian community both in Edinburgh and Glasgow.

After being established in Edinburgh, Mama Evelyn had become a well-respected figure within that community. For several years she was elected either president or chair of a few Asian associations and had been frequently involved in charitable works ever since she moved to the UK. It was a no brainer for Mr Walker to ensure he had a solid and pleasant relationship with Evelyn Wang. No one knew how it came about, but Evelyn also became quite a successful matchmaker for the Asian communities, as she was both well connected and well known, though none of her three children appreciated her meddling in their love lives and interests.

Mr Walker's business flourished within the Asian community, thanks to word of mouth and with the recommendations of Mama Evelyn. Whether it was about finding a residential home, business, mortgage, insurance or renovation work, you name it,

Mr Walker and Andrew were able to meet their needs and demands.

Looking back, Andrew didn't know how he had managed to juggle work, take care of Nathan, and complete a few evening class diplomas in interior design and business management. Andrew also invested in properties; renovating and selling them on, financing this from the money Hilary had given him after selling the corner shop.

Eventually, Mr Walker retired and sold the business to Andrew. Mr Walker moved to Spain with his wife to be near one of their daughters, who had married a Spanish businessman. Not long after retiring, Mr Walker grew restless and started an estate agency in Spain with his son-in-law, focusing mainly on helping British customers who wanted to buy properties in Spain.

Andrew and Nathan were invited several times to visit Mr Walker in Spain, especially when Mr Walker got married again. Mr Walker's wife died unexpectedly in the second year after their move to Spain. When he remarried three years later, to a British widow living there, Andrew was the best man at his wedding.

When Nathan was eight years old, Andrew was doing quite well and bought himself and Nathan a place in the West End of Edinburgh and moved out of Hilary's home. Hilary was both proud and pleased for Andrew and what he had achieved, but she was familiar with tough times, having raised him as a single mother; apart from being humble, she had always taught Andrew to be grateful to the people who had helped them.

"Forgive someone that has been mean to you and remember to learn something from it and never forget a person who lends you a helping hand," Andrew passed on his mother's words to Nathan. But it was Mama Evelyn's proudly spoken, wise and witty words on the philosophy of life that brought a smile to Andrew's face when at times he needed cheering up.

"Andrew, listen to Mama Evelyn. It is harder to reach something when you have started from nothing." She also loved to say, "One should never argue or disagree with a woman when she is hungry."

Mama Evelyn loved shopping in the sales, especially for shoes and bags. Although Mama Evelyn was a wealthy woman, she almost never took taxis during her shopping trips. She often came back to the restaurant exhausted but excited by these excursions. She would come in fully laden with shopping bags filled with her bargain finds.

"Mama Evelyn, why don't you take a taxi?" Andrew asked, while he and Jimi gave her a back and neck massage after one of her shopping adventures. Andrew never understood why Mama Evelyn would torture herself by carrying all those bags to the point of making it so painful.

"Andrew, you see, I always believe that if one can shop, then one should be able to carry. So, no taxi for me." She smiled as she pulled out the bags and showed everyone her great finds.

Having established himself as a well-known, edgy interior designer with a good reputation, Andrew sold his agency to a bigger chain and opened an interior design workshop. Apart from meeting clients and carrying out inspections at sites, he mainly worked from home, so he had more time to take care of Nathan. At one point he owned ten properties in addition to the one he and Nathan lived in. He was able to support himself and Nathan from the rental revenues, plus he had the income from his interior design and renovation work for other clients.

Andrew was well known for incorporating Feng Shui principles into his work, which he had learnt from Mama Evelyn and from attending seminars in London and self-study. He also continued writing about food, and a few of his articles and recipes were published in mainstream magazines.

Thanks to hard work, determination, dedication and a lot of luck coming his way, Andrew was finally able to achieve the financial security he had been striving for. The driving force was, of course, to provide a comfortable life for his son Nathan.

Chapter 6
Nathan's Upbringing

Hilary and Nathan adored each other. From the first moment Hilary saw Nathan, a special bond was formed, and she protected him while showering him with all her grandmotherly love. Hilary enjoyed being that special person in Nathan's life.

Nathan and Andrew moved out when Nathan was about eight, but Nathan continued to see his grandmother almost daily and loved accompanying her on shopping trips and having meals alone with her. It seemed that Nathan's role in life was firstly to be his grandmother's grandson and secondly to be a son to Lena and Andrew.

When Nathan first came home from hospital, as Lena hadn't been able to take care of him and Andrew was inexperienced, little baby Nathan slept in Hilary's room. Hilary comforted and cuddled Nathan when he would often cry non-stop for hours for no apparent reason. She fed, bathed and looked after him, though she did try to encourage Lena to be more involved with the care of the baby.

After Lena went back to Sweden for the first few years of Nathan's life, Andrew, Hilary and Mama Evelyn cared for Nathan in Edinburgh; but Lena frequently came to visit, and Nathan spent time in Sweden with Lena's family as well.

Lena and Andrew were blessed. Although they didn't function as a couple, they were always on good terms with each other and their focus was always on what was best for Nathan. After returning to Sweden, Lena continued her studies and became a child counsellor. She later met a man, Leif, and had two children with him. Nathan loved travelling to Sweden and spending time with his mother and half-siblings.

When Nathan was three, Lena wanted to have Nathan with her full time, so he only came back to Edinburgh when it was time to start his primary education. It was Hilary who taught him how to behave and how to protect himself from rude or mean kids when he first started school. Mama Evelyn added that if anyone was mean to him, he should remember their names and she and Hilary would sort them out.

Andrew knew nothing of this arrangement until Nathan's teacher contacted him and told him that Nathan had proudly told other pupils that his grandmothers would beat them up if they messed with him. His fellow pupils told their parents, who then contacted the school. Andrew was called in to explain.

Luckily, after he talked with the school, the complaints were not taken further. The two 'hooligans' responsible told Andrew how innocent they were and that they hadn't told Nathan anything of the sort; but Andrew was still furious and had to refrain from shouting at Hilary and Mama Evelyn. He wanted them to realise how serious it was, and he told them both to stop putting strange ideas into Nathan's head.

Nathan might not have been the most textbook-smart pupil in the class or the one who got the best grades, but he was bright and a quick learner. It might have had something to do with having to learn two languages from birth. When he first started talking, he would say things that neither Andrew nor Hilary understood. When they phoned Lena, asking her to translate, she wasn't able to grasp it either. It took a while, but later they discovered that Nathan had formed his own language; neither Swedish nor English, but a combination of the two. It was Nathan's language.

Nathan always received positive remarks and reports from his teachers; in particular, he was interested in learning new subjects and often asked "why?" He wanted to know the reasons; whereas most of the kids just accepted what they were being taught by their teachers. Andrew also learned from

Nathan's teacher that he wasn't afraid to stand up for other kids, even if it meant putting himself in a difficult situation.

He was attentive to others and outgoing at the same time. He wasn't shy of making presentations in front of the class. He was also good at maths and loved languages; he was bi-lingual and additionally spoke basic conversational Cantonese, having spent so much time with Mama Evelyn and Sami.

Like his mother, Nathan was blond and had amazing blue eyes. He was a beautiful adorable little boy.

In Hilary and Mama Evelyn's eyes, Nathan could do no wrong, even if he tried. For Hilary, Nathan was the most perfect child in the whole world, while Mama Evelyn would have let Nathan get away with murder. Andrew didn't consider himself a strict father, but he didn't want Nathan to be spoiled. Nathan was lucky to have so many people in his life that loved him. He was fortunate to grow up in and experience two different cultures, flying frequently to Sweden, visiting Lena and Leif and Lena's family during the summer, Easter and Christmas holidays. Andrew taught him not to take things for granted, and Nathan was grounded and respectful towards others, especially the elderly. He loved spending time with Hilary, Mama Evelyn and Lena's parents, and was kind and caring towards his half-brother and sister.

Though Lena and Andrew weren't in constant contact, they did communicate well regarding Nathan's upbringing and both agreed Nathan shouldn't be spoiled. But maybe it was her guilt about leaving Nathan to be brought up by Andrew and Hilary that led Lena to be much more lenient towards him. While Nathan was taught to believe that he was special to them, from an early age he was made aware of the importance of humility; he needed to be accountable for his actions and be responsible in terms of schoolwork and assignments.

There was only one thing Andrew and Nathan constantly argued and fought about — Nathan's untidiness. He was messy. Whenever he was in the kitchen, Andrew had to tidy up after him. No matter what Andrew said, or how often he said it, Nathan hardly ever cleaned his room, either leaving his dirty smelly socks lying everywhere or piles of clothes on the floor. Andrew wanted him to be more independent; so, starting from when he was about fifteen, Andrew told him that he had to do his own laundry. Surprisingly, Nathan always had clean clothes on. However, one day, to his horror and embarrassment, Andrew learned that Nathan didn't change his bed linen for about six months at a time. He told Andrew, "I just didn't think about it," and then looked at him as if wondering why he had made it such a big deal.

When Nathan was sixteen, he started talking about a one-year exchange student programme in the USA for the last year of high school. Lena and Andrew had no idea how much Nathan struggled before finding the courage to ask them if it were possible for him to find out more and then apply. One day at school, right after his seventeenth birthday, he and his schoolmates passed by the noticeboard in the hallway outside the lunch-room. Some students were talking and pointing at a poster.

"Hey, did you see that poster about studying in the USA for a year as an exchange student?" One of his mates came to the table where they were all sitting and told them about the poster he had seen on the way in. A few of them were interested in the idea of studying and living in the USA for a year or were thinking how cool it would be to live in the USA with a host family, away from their families.

Nathan didn't pay much attention to the conversation, as his thoughts were 'It's not for me. I wouldn't be able to be away from my family for so long and be so far away.' Not to mention he realised how sad his grandmother would be, and he had totally dismissed the idea by the time he got home.

That night, Nathan woke from his sleep with a sudden revelation. 'Why not? Why couldn't I go?' It was the first rebellious idea he had ever conceived, and it scared him a little. Nathan couldn't go back to sleep, and he started to think about his life. He had been very protected so far; he was loved and nurtured by his grandmother, his father, his mother, his maternal grandparents and even by the Wang family. That night, for the first time, Nathan felt claustrophobic and had an urge to break free from this protection and love. It was the world he knew, but at times he found it overbearing, with everyone treating him as special. Thinking about getting away from it all immediately made him feel guilty.

Over the next few days he tried not to think about it, but a voice inside kept asking him, 'Why not? Why can't I explore and find out more?'

"Sami, can I see you? I need to talk to you." As they had practically grown up together, Sami was like a big sister to him and the only person Nathan felt comfortable sharing his thoughts with. Nathan called Sami's brothers Uncle Joey and Uncle Jimi, but for him Sami was just Sami.

They met in a café on a Saturday afternoon and Nathan told her about the exchange programme and his doubts. "Well, Nathan, I'm privileged that you trust me enough to share this with me. I'm extremely proud of you wanting to take on new challenges."

"I don't know, I just feel torn and guilty even thinking about leaving everyone."

"Nathan, you have to do what you feel is right for you. I know your family; most of all, your

71

grandmother would be very sad not having you here for such a long time. Wait! But it's not even for a year. It's August to June." Sami carefully read the small brochure Nathan had handed to her.

"I just feel that I want to explore the possibility." Nathan's eyes brightened up as he felt he had Sami's support.

"I'm not saying you should go or you shouldn't go, but I think you should at least give yourself a chance to discuss it with your parents and find out more about the programme." Sami tenderly looked at Nathan.

"Do you think they would be angry with me?"

"Why would they be angry with you? It's not like you are moving to the moon forever!" They both laughed.

Nathan waited a few more days after he had talked to Sami. He called Lena first and then told Andrew about the exchange programme. Andrew was a bit taken aback by the idea, but later he was very proud of Nathan for wanting to explore new avenues and take chances in his life. Maybe Andrew was happy for Nathan doing the things he wasn't able to do when he was Nathan's age.

Andrew remembered an incident when Nathan was about eleven or twelve. Andrew was supposed to fly with him to Sweden to visit Lena and her family, but Andrew came down with bad flu and was unable to fly. There were many suggestions as to how to get Nathan to Sweden, and finally Lena and Andrew made a special arrangement with the airline, to have a staff member accompany him on the journey and Lena collect him on arrival.

Andrew didn't tell Hilary about it, as she would never have allowed Nathan to travel alone. The flight attendant told Lena upon arrival when Lena came to meet him at the airport that Nathan wasn't shy or afraid at all. He spoke to an elderly lady sitting next to him and told her about why he was travelling alone to Sweden. It was then that Andrew realised that Nathan enjoyed his independence and liked to explore new adventures of his own.

Andrew discussed it with Lena and luckily, they were financially able to send him to the USA. They both thought about it and agreed that it would be a good opportunity for Nathan to have this experience in his life.

Hilary wasn't so keen on the idea of Nathan living with a totally unknown family in the USA for a whole school year. Additionally, she worried that when Nathan came back, he might have to repeat the missing year of education in Edinburgh, and all his other friends and classmates would have already gone on ahead of him. In the end, Andrew let Nathan speak to his grandmother himself, as he knew it was better and easier if they talked about it; and, of course, he convinced her.

A few months after the initial application and interview, they received an approval and an email describing Nathan's host family in Upstate New York. Both Nathan and Andrew communicated by email and phone with his host family, Mark and Linda Harper. They had two young children and it was their first time hosting an exchange student. They had visited Europe when they were first married.

Before Nathan left for the USA, he prepared a table full of Swedish specialities, including herrings and crayfish that he had brought back from Sweden on his latest trip there, and he invited Andrew, Hilary, Mama Evelyn, Sami and Jimi over for dinner. Jimi was already working in Geneva at that time and had come back especially, to spend time with Nathan in Edinburgh before his trip.

Nathan had done everything, the design of the menu, the shopping for the ingredients, the cooking and the laying of the table. He was so proud and excited and everyone was impressed, especially his grandmother.

Mama Evelyn made a special effort to eat the whole meal using a knife and fork, though she whispered to Andrew, "It would've been easier to eat the Swedish meatballs with chopsticks."

"Have you seen the state of the kitchen and the mess Nathan's made?" whispered Andrew back to Mama Evelyn who sat next to him. "I am sure I am the one who will have to clean it up." They both smiled and chuckled discreetly.

Hilary missed Nathan terribly after he had left; and, truth be told, so did Andrew. It was the first time Andrew had lived in his and Nathan's home by himself for such a long period of time. Luckily, they were able to email and Skype. This was when Andrew introduced Skype to Hilary so she could see Nathan when they talked. Throughout the year they learned that Nathan was getting along well with his host family and their kids and had made good friends at school.

He also became good friends with a neighbour's kid called Justin, who was the same age as Nathan, and they went to the same school. Nathan and Justin joined the school choir and performed at various functions in nearby cities for competitions and charitable causes. Nathan visited Washington DC, Atlantic City and Connecticut with the school choir and on school trips. Nathan also went to Disneyland with Mark and Linda and their kids.

Andrew also learned from Lena that Nathan had met a girl called Olivia. She was from Glasgow and had entered the same exchange programme as Nathan, though she had been assigned to a different high school. They met often, as both lived in Upstate New York with their host families. Andrew didn't tell Hilary about Olivia, as he wasn't sure how serious their relationship was and didn't dare to imagine Hilary's reaction. He thought it was best for Nathan to break the news to her himself if, and when, he was ready.

With so many activities going on in his life, sometimes Andrew wondered if Nathan had any time for his studies. Although, deep down Andrew was very pleased for Nathan being able to have this incredible chance in his life.

Driving lessons were another big event for Nathan. Mark emailed Andrew one day asking for permission to teach Nathan how to drive. Of course, replied Andrew with gratitude. He appreciated how difficult it can be to teach someone in your own family how to drive.

Andrew was eating dinner with Hilary and Mama Evelyn in her restaurant when the phone rang; it was Nathan. "Dad, I got my driver's licence! I got my driver's licence!" Nathan screamed so loudly that even Hilary and Mama Evelyn could hear.

"Congratulations, I'm very proud of you," Andrew said with enthusiasm, and continued, "Don't forget to thank Mark for teaching you. I'm having dinner with your grandmother and Mama Evelyn." When Andrew looked around, he saw Hilary wasn't amused and looked worried, so he passed her the phone.

"Nathan, please be careful. I heard that people drive very fast in the States." Hilary sounded really worried.

"Nan, don't worry. I don't have a car and will only borrow Mark's car now and again to practise. Are you guys having dinner? What are you having? Please send my regards to Mama Evelyn." Nathan wanted to calm his grandmother down, so he diffused the situation by telling her about his school and his trips to Disneyland in Florida with Mark, Linda and their kids. After they ended the conversation, Hilary handed the phone back to Andrew.

"Nathan is too young to drive," Hilary voiced her fear.

"Yes, too young to drive," echoed Mama Evelyn in agreement.

"Listen," Andrew said, looking at them both, "he does not have a car, so he won't be driving often. He will only borrow Mark's car from time to time to practise and gain experience. Don't worry. He'll be fine." Andrew really didn't know what else to say to reassure them and calm them down.

Then Andrew's phone rang again; it was Lena. "I just got off the phone with Nathan. Has he told you that he's got his driver's licence?"

"Yes, I'm proud of him, especially since I've never learned how to drive myself." Andrew wasn't sure how happy Lena was about the news, so he waited for her to continue.

"He talked about maybe buying a car when he goes back to the USA in the fall for university, but I told him that we should discuss it first when he's back home…"

Andrew interrupted her, as he didn't want to lead to another topic that he knew his mother was not happy about. "Lena, I'm having dinner with my mum and Mama Evelyn. I'll call you once I'm home."

Since Nathan was enjoying the USA and doing so well in school, he talked to Lena and Andrew about returning to the States for university, instead of studying in Edinburgh. Lena and Andrew talked about it at length over the phone and were not convinced at first, but were unable to come up with a reason as to why it wouldn't be a good opportunity for Nathan. The plan was that Nathan would apply to a community college first, as it would be easier to get into while staying with Mark and Linda; later, he would transfer to a state college somewhere.

Of course, Hilary wasn't pleased about it, but she refrained from expressing her disappointment; she didn't want to be the one to hinder the progress of Nathan's studies and future. However, Andrew knew she felt a sense of loss and abandonment. What

Andrew hadn't told her was that, as a surprise to celebrate her sixtieth birthday, he planned to take her to visit Nathan in the States once he'd settled down at university.

Though Nathan didn't come home for Christmas, much to Hilary's dismay, the almost ten months he spent there went quite swiftly. They were able to follow his stay through his Facebook pictures and postings, and they spoke frequently on the phone and via Skype. Two weeks before his return, he posted a picture on Facebook — it was his high school diploma. Andrew showed it to Hilary and he thought no one would ever be able to wipe away the smile from the proud grandmother's face.

A week before his return, Hilary and Mama Evelyn had already started planning all the things they wanted to do with Nathan when he got back, and they had stocked their pantries with all his favourite food, treats and snacks. Secretly, Andrew did the same.

Hilary, Mama Evelyn, Sami and Andrew waited in the airport with a welcome-home banner that Hilary and Sami had spent hours making the night before. "Please behave, and no shouting," Andrew told the three women to try not to embarrass Nathan too much in the airport once he got out. But as soon as they caught sight of him, they all jumped and hugged him and cried with joy.

Nathan spent the first few nights in Edinburgh at his grandmother's place. It seemed as if they never ran out of subjects to talk about. He worked a few days in Mama Evelyn's restaurant in order to spend time with his grandmother and Mama Evelyn. Mama Evelyn wanted to pay him for his hours; but, of course, Nathan refused. In return, Mama Evelyn asked him to invite a few of his good friends from school over to the restaurant and treated them to a banquet.

Nathan had been born when Sami was about ten. When growing up, Nathan didn't have siblings or cousins in Scotland, so Sami was like a big sister to him and Nathan looked up to her. As Sami was the youngest in her family, she was thrilled to have Nathan as her little brother. They never needed to hire and pay for a babysitter; Sami often watched over him when others were busy. She enjoyed looking after Nathan when he was little; Nathan was her living doll. Sami and Nathan were also the best playmates.

So, in order for them to be able to spend some quality time together, just the two of them, Sami treated Nathan to a weekend in London. They took the train down to London together and were able to have time to talk. Nathan shared with Sami his plans for his studies and he also talked about Olivia.

Hilary was quite happy to know that Nathan had a girlfriend and had asked Nathan to invite Olivia to come to Edinburgh. She and Mama Evelyn couldn't have been more welcoming to Olivia the few times she came to visit. Actually, it was Andrew who felt awkward and uneasy at first, especially the first time Olivia spent the night with Nathan in their flat.

Andrew was anxious and called Jimi for advice when he learned the first time Nathan had invited Olivia to stay over. "Do you think I need to have a father-to-son talk with Nathan? Or, maybe it is best that it comes from you?"

"To talk about what?" Jimi had no idea what Andrew was referring to.

Andrew explained his worries. "I am not ready to become a grandfather yet."

"Don't be daft, and don't say anything. You are going to embarrass him. Nathan knows what he is doing. Grandad Andrew!" Jimi teased and chuckled.

Andrew guessed he was just not used to seeing his son as a grown-up young man. For Andrew, Nathan was and always would be his child. He was also worried about what if, for some reason, they didn't like each other.

When Olivia finally came to stay, Andrew realised he needn't have been concerned. She was well mannered, cheerful and respectful. She was easy going and fussed over Nathan as subtly as any girl could. Their relationship was obviously more serious than Andrew had thought; they were visibly in love and also good friends. At first, Andrew thought about staying in a hotel to give them space, but was worried about leaving them totally alone as well. The next morning, as they came out of Nathan's bedroom, Andrew didn't know how to act or what to say, so he just prepared breakfast for them and pretended that he was okay with it.

Olivia went with Nathan's plan to continue his university studies in the USA, and they got into the same community college. Lena, Hilary and Andrew were all pleased to know that Nathan was not returning to the USA by himself and that he would be staying with Mark and Linda for the first few months.

Nathan also flew to Sweden to visit Lena and the extended family and stayed there for three weeks. While he was in Sweden, he visited Lena's parents at their summerhouse as well. He came back to Edinburgh with a suitcase full of Swedish delicacies and new clothes Lena and his grandparents had bought for him.

During his stay there, Lena and Leif got married. They had been living together for many years and just decided to tie the knot. Nathan was so proud to walk down the aisle with Lena and handed her over to Leif. Unfortunately, Lena's father was too old and too ill to do so, but they knew how much it meant to Lena and Nathan.

When he got back, Nathan showed Andrew, Hilary and Mama Evelyn the pictures of his visit and the wedding. It was the first time he had dressed in a proper dinner jacket and bow-tie. He was a handsome, striking young man. "You look like a waiter," Andrew teased, pointing at the photos. Although in his heart he could not have been prouder. His son looked stunning and truly happy.

"Hush," said Mama Evelyn, jumping in before Hillary was able to say something. Mama Evelyn glanced at Andrew with the pretence of an angry frown.

"Don't listen to your father. He's just envious because he wasn't invited to the wedding." Hilary joined in to support Mama Evelyn in order to defend Nathan. Also, Hilary knew that the dinner jacket had been bought by Lena and she wanted Nathan to know how good he looked in it. Actually, both Hilary and Andrew had been invited to the wedding, but they had decided not to go; they wanted this occasion to be a special one for Nathan and Lena's family.

Naturally, Hilary and Mama Evelyn were both proud and thrilled for Nathan and weren't able to stop praising him. "Don't forget to give us a copy of the photos, especially this one." Both Hilary and Mama Evelyn pointed to a picture where Nathan, dressed in his dinner jacket, stood outside the church right after the wedding. The sun shone on Nathan's golden hair. With his eyes shining with pride, he had that hint of cockiness that only young people have; as if everything was possible. Why shouldn't it be? Nathan was eighteen at that time, with all his life before him.

No one could have imagined in their wildest dreams that those were to be the last photos of Nathan with his mother, half-siblings and the extended family.

Six months after the pictures were taken, Nathan was lying in a coffin; dressed in the same dinner jacket Lena had bought for him to wear at her wedding.

Chapter 7
Jimi's Underwear

Ten days before Nathan and Olivia were due to return to the USA to start university, Jimi invited Nathan and Andrew to visit him for a week in Geneva.

"It's my graduation present for Nathan. I can't wait to spend some time with you both and show you around," Jimi told Andrew over the phone, insisting, "Don't argue with me. I've already bought your tickets."

Jimi hadn't seen Nathan for more than a year, so as soon as he saw them both coming out of Customs, he ran up to Nathan and gave him a huge hug.

"Wow, Nathan! You're a grown man! I hear you've got yourself a girlfriend." Jimi took a closer look at Nathan and then teased him by messing with his hair.

Nathan blushed. "It's great to see you, Uncle Jimi. Thanks for inviting us. The last time I saw you was when you came to the Swedish dinner party I organised before I left for the USA last year."

"Hi there, it's really great to see you." Andrew approached Jimi and also gave him a hug.

It was a beautiful summer's day in Geneva and as Jimi drove them to his place, Andrew and Nathan were both impressed at the sight of the mountains. Nathan sat in the front with Jimi. "Uncle Jimi, what mountains are these?"

"Looking straight ahead you can see the Salève, and further away over there is Mont Blanc. Behind you, you can see the Jura mountain chain. If we have time, we'll drive up there for lunch one day." Jimi said it in such a way as if it were the most normal thing in the world.

He owned a beautiful penthouse in the central part of Geneva, very close to Lake Geneva. He showed them around his three-bedroom flat; there were two terraces, one in the back, where you could see Mont Blanc, and the other just outside the living room, where you could see a glimpse of Lake Geneva.

Both Nathan and Andrew were very impressed. Andrew looked at Jimi and asked, "Wow! Who lives like this? So happy for you; you've done so well."

As an interior designer himself, Andrew noticed the quality and finesse in Jimi's flat, the lighting, the polished original wooden floor, the under-floor heating in all the bathrooms (yes, plural), the bright windows and skylights in all the rooms, his display of decorative items, the colour combinations and co-ordination. Jimi's furniture was a mixture of

European and Oriental pieces. As he walked around, Andrew felt there was a good Feng Shui energy inside the flat. Mama Evelyn would have been proud.

For Andrew, it was all well-co-ordinated and decorated, but the thing that made him laugh was the excessive number of mirrors, everywhere.

Jimi then showed them the "bargains and special finds" that he had found at an auction he went to once a week. It was a mostly tasteful collection, but there were some gauche crystal, porcelains and oil paintings. Andrew made a discrete gesture to Nathan not to comment on anything when Jimi wasn't noticing.

It seemed that Jimi had endless places to show them; Geneva and its surrounding cities were just as beautiful as on the postcards, if not more so. During the week they had a BBQ a few times on his terrace overlooking Lake Geneva; they visited Chamonix, where they had lunch and saw glaciers and the mountains of Mont Blanc; they drove to Lausanne and visited the Olympic Museum, and then took a boat over to Evian for lunch. They spent a whole afternoon in Evian Spa; they also visited the United Nations and the Red Cross.

One evening, Jimi invited a number of his colleagues and friends over for dinner. His flat was packed with people; most of them were women. As usual, he was very popular and mingled smoothly amongst them. He was like a magnet, and everyone was just drawn to him and listened to what he had to say.

There were so many names, but Andrew remembered one guy in particular because he was very attentive and helped Jimi a lot in the kitchen. His name was Vincent.

As Jimi was busy in the kitchen and mingling with guests, Andrew acted as the waiter, serving finger-food, and Nathan helped out refilling the guests' glasses with wine and champagne. Andrew watched him for a while and saw that Nathan mixed well with the guests, and no one's glass was ever empty. He smiled and felt proud of his son.

The party was a success and everyone who chatted to Nathan thought that he was charming and sweet. He spoke Swedish to Jimi's colleagues from Scandinavia and, most unexpectedly for the guests, he also spoke quite a few full Cantonese sentences to Jimi's friends from Hong Kong, which impressed them immensely.

Jimi came out from the kitchen from time to time to check on his guests and at one point he pulled Nathan to him and proudly declared to everyone, "This is my godson. This is my godson." Jimi messed up Nathan's hair. Nathan hadn't actually been baptised, but Jimi had considered himself to be Nathan's godfather from the day Nathan was born.

The party lasted till two in the morning, and once everyone had left, and realising how exhausted they all were, Jimi, Nathan and Andrew lay down on the outdoor sofa on the terrace.

"What a lovely evening. Which of those women did you fancy, Uncle Jimi?" asked Nathan. As Jimi was about to answer, he and Andrew both looked at Nathan, who apparently was a bit tipsy. It was the first time Andrew had seen Nathan drinking alcohol and getting drunk in front of him.

Seeing the look on Andrew's face, and worried that he might say something to Nathan, Jimi stood up, patting Andrew's shoulder, and as he went inside, he said, "Oh, lighten up! Don't be such a party pooper. Wait here."

Jimi came back out and handed a bag to Nathan. "Here, congratulations! This is a graduation gift for you." Nathan sat up straight and looked at his father for approval whether to accept the gift or not.

"Jimi, this is too much, you've already done a lot for us this week."

Jimi smiled, moved and sat next to Nathan. "This is between me and my godson. Open it." Nathan took out the box inside the bag; it was a Tissot watch. Both Nathan and Andrew were stunned by Jimi's generosity. Nathan put the watch on, suddenly appearing dapper and grown-up.

"Thank you, Uncle Jimi." He gave Jimi a huge hug and Andrew could see tears in both their eyes.

"It is a new watch and I bought it in an auction," Jimi said, after they had composed themselves. "We are going there tomorrow afternoon."

Jokingly Andrew rolled his eyes and chuckled. "Yes, as one does on a Sunday afternoon."

They continued chatting till Andrew realised that Nathan had fallen asleep. He asked Jimi for a blanket to put over Nathan, as it was getting a bit breezy. Looking at the sky full of stars and then checking on Nathan, Andrew asked quietly, as he didn't want to wake up Nathan. "How is work? You seem to do important humanitarian work."

"Well, I like my work and, as you say, there are important humanitarian aspects to it, but I'm tired and not good at office politics. And I'm really frustrated with the corruption and sometimes I feel totally powerless."

"What kind of politics and corruption?"

"Once, I represented a world food programme agency and interviewed prisoners in an underdeveloped country. The living conditions for these prisoners were horrendous. You can't imagine the smell, the thick air, the heat and the limited space they were in. The guards often beat them for no reason, and one young man I spoke to didn't even know why the police had put him there." Jimi paused as he tried to recall the event.

"In the prisoners' kitchen another young man pointed at all the rice bags we had sent, and as the guards were busy talking to my other colleagues, he whispered to me and said, "They told you this rice will be cooked for us, but they are just for show. When you are gone the guards will take them home to their families. We are allowed two scoops of boiled barley a day." Then he pointed at a tiny broken spoon. I was stunned by what I saw. There's no way they could be full with that small amount of food.

"When I went back to the office, I reported this to my supervisor, but was told not to get involved, as it might have made the prisoners' conditions even worse."

Jimi looked over and ensured Nathan was sound asleep before he lit a cigarette. He offered one to Andrew, but Andrew just smiled and shook his head.

"In the office people are always fighting for a chance to get promoted. You'd not believe what people will do to get ahead. Colleagues became friends because they had people they didn't like in common, not because they actually liked each other." Jimi sounded frustrated.

"That is horrible. I work for myself these days and I used to work in a small office and had only one boss," said Andrew, thinking of his previous boss, Mr

Walker. "I'm not sure I am cut out for work in a large organisation or institution."

They were both silent for a few moments. Jimi went inside and came back with two glasses of gin and tonic. "Here." He handed one to Andrew. He went back in again and this time returned with blankets for them both.

"A promotion came up once and a colleague, who was at the same level as everyone in the unit, told us all we weren't qualified, so there was no point in applying. He'd also heard that the position was already assigned to an external candidate from another UN agency. In the end no one from our unit applied, except for him; he got the job and became our supervisor." Jimi sighed. "Can you fucking believe it!" Jimi let out a strange laugh and Andrew laughed along with him.

Unconsciously, they both yawned at the same time, looked at each other and chuckled quietly so as not to wake up Nathan.

"God, I'm tired." Andrew yawned again.

"Me, too." Continued Jimmy, yawning in sympathy. "I've thought about leaving my job so many times, selling my flat here and moving somewhere to do God knows what, but something totally different."

"Why don't you! I'm sure you'll do something great, whatever you set your mind to." That was the last thing Andrew remembered saying before they fell asleep under blankets on that breezy summer night under the beautiful stars, outside on the terrace of Jimi's penthouse near Lake Geneva.

At that time no one would have guessed that a few years later, after the conversation they had that night, Jimi handed in his notice at work and sold his flat in Geneva. With the help of Andrew's former boss, Mr Walker, Jimi bought a large mansion in Spain, which he renovated and turned into a high-end boutique bed and breakfast for exclusive clientele, and ran it with his partner.

At that time no one would have anticipated either that it would be the last time the three of them would be spending time together.

After they woke up the next morning, Andrew made fun of Jimi's snoring, until Jimi had finally had it.

"I don't want to burst your bubble, but you snored like a pig last night."

"I don't snore." Andrew's face turned red and was genuinely surprised to hear that. "Do I snore?" he asked, and looked at Nathan for confirmation, but even more for support.

Nathan wasn't able to meet his dad's intense stare, so he didn't say a word, but shyly and awkwardly nodded his head, hoping he didn't embarrass his dad too much. They all laughed hysterically.

"I really don't snore." Andrew was in denial and still insisted his "innocence" and blamed it on being drunk after the last gin and tonic Jimi had given him, which made Jimi and Nathan laugh even harder.

They had a late brunch before Jimi took Andrew and Nathan to the auction house, which was not that far away. "We'll have time to take a quick look through the items to be auctioned this afternoon."

"Please be careful not to raise your hand during the auction," Andrew said jokingly to Nathan, who made a facial expression, not finding Andrew's remark amusing.

Jimi seemed to know a lot of people there as he kept greeting everyone, both the customers and staff members. One of the male staff members approached Jimi and gave him a wooden bidding sign. "Mr Wang, you are number 72 today."

"Thanks. Could you please reserve three seats for us today?" Jimi indicated the three of them with the bidding sign.

Jimi walked around the showroom and pointed to a few paintings and furniture items he thought were interesting. He stopped in front of a rather tall porcelain statue. "How unusual. Normally Guanyin wears a white or light blue robe, but this one wears red." He lifted up the porcelain figurine and turned it over to see the mark and maker. "Oh, this is not an antique and it was not made to a high quality." Jimi put it down and continued showing them some of the luxury jewellery items that he said he would love to have but were just too expensive. They sat down; the auction was about to start.

For the first two hours there were expensive wines, books and paintings that all went under the hammer. Andrew had visited auction houses a few times before and had purchased items for himself and on behalf of his clients, but this was the first time for Nathan. He was impressed and asked Jimi lots of questions about the bidding procedures.

Then, the slots for porcelains and crystals started. There were a few interesting pieces and Jimi took part in the bidding, but didn't get any; his bids were slightly too low.

Finally, the Guanyin figurine was shown on the screen. The auctioneer shouted out a price, but there were no bids. In order to generate interest, he lowered the price — still no interest. His third attempt, asking a very low amount, was more successful; even Jimi raised his bidding sign. "At this low price it is worth buying, even just as a modern decorative item," Jimi looked at them and whispered quietly to both.

As a few people started raising their signs, the price of the item started going up. Jimi raised his sign a second time and the price went up even further; then even more people raised their signs. "Oh, what the hell." Jimi raised his bidding sign again.

As people saw him raise his sign three times, for a moment it seemed that everyone was looking at him and time stood still. The next moment, the three of them realised that almost half of the customers in the sales-room had raised their signs. In the end, the figurine was sold to someone at a price four times the original highest recommended price. Jimi looked stunned. After a few more items were auctioned, and without any explanation, Jimi told Andrew and Nathan that it was time for them to leave.

They left quietly, and as soon as they were outside and had passed a few shops, Jimi started laughing and started to run very fast, like a careless child. Nathan and Andrew just followed, and as they caught up with him Andrew asked, "What? What happened? Why did we have to leave?"

Jimi bent down to catch his breath. "Blimey, since I am well-known there, and just because I'm Asian, they must have thought I knew something about that figurine. Because I raised my bid three times, they must have assumed it was valuable. The buyer is going to kill me when he finds out that it was only a modern decorative item. I'm not going back there again." He then laughed and laughed till he almost choked.

After a while, Jimi calmed down and Andrew told him that he wanted to cook dinner that evening and it would be nice just chilling out and eating at home for their last night together. He promised Jimi and Nathan an Asian feast. They went to an Asian supermarket in town to purchase most of the ingredients, as Jimi didn't know how to cook Asian food and had almost no Asian ingredients at home. He didn't even own a rice cooker.

When they got home, Andrew went straight into the kitchen and Nathan talked to Olivia via Skype. "Time has passed by so quickly. He has a girlfriend now!" said Jimi, coming into the kitchen to help set the table.

"I know, we're getting old," Andrew replied, busily pan-frying the noodles and prawns in oyster sauce.

"Speak for yourself," Jimi continued, "we're not even forty, and by the way, forty is the new thirty," he argued, with a cheeky smile on his face.

Nathan came into the kitchen. "Anything I can help with?"

Andrew pointed to all the dishes. "Put all these on the table and go and sit down. I'll bring out the boiled rice."

During dinner Jimi told Nathan about his recent travels for work abroad, visiting prisons and interviewing prisoners. Nathan was impressed and amazed by his experiences.

"Nathan, you should consider majoring in international relations. It might open up a lot of doors for you." Jimi looked at them both.

"As it's my first year in community college, I'll start studying business administration, and when I transfer to New York State University I'll really reconsider my major," said Nathan.

"Good plan," approved Jimi proudly.

After dinner Jimi gave them instructions on how and where to leave his keys as their return flight was at two p.m., he would be at work and he would be away for two days for a meeting, returning Tuesday evening.

"Put the keys in an envelope and leave it in my mailbox downstairs," he said.

"Are you sure?" Andrew wasn't comfortable with the idea, worried that other people might have access to the mailbox area.

"Don't worry about it. I've done it loads of times before when I've had visitors," he assured Andrew, and then handed him an envelope.

"Now, do you want to see my fetish collection?" said Jimi with a mysterious smile.

Nathan first looked at Andrew and then asked, "Uncle Jimi, what is your collection?"

Jimi stood up and led them to his walk-in closet joined to his en-suite bedroom. "Ta-da!" Like a naughty child, he gestured with a wave of his hand after he had opened the closet and there they were, an impressive one hundred boxes or more of expensive and branded designer men's underwear.

"Oh, my goodness, Jimi, you're mad." Andrew was rather surprised that one person could own so many pairs of underpants, and the weirdest thing was that they were still new and in their original packaging.

"Well, wherever I travel to, instead of buying trashy and useless souvenirs that were made in China anyway, I buy a few pairs of men's underwear."

Nathan and Andrew were like two kids in a candy store looking through them. Jimi picked up a few boxes and handed them over to Nathan. "Here, Nathan. I'm sure you can wear these, as we are the only two with a thirty-inch waist here," said Jimi, proudly adding that he watched what he ate and went to the gym regularly. "Your father, on the other hand, I am not so sure," Jimi teased.

"Ha, ha, very funny. I have more muscles than you do. You're going to spoil him." Andrew looked at Nathan and then looked back at Jimi.

"Uncle Jimi, are you sure? These are very expensive." Nathan recognised the brands and knew how much they cost and wasn't comfortable accepting them.

"Please stop all this drama. We're not going to cry again, are we?" Jimi hugged Nathan and told him to try to do well in his studies.

The next morning, Andrew woke up early and made breakfast for Jimi while Jimi was taking a shower. Not wanting to disturb Nathan, they ate breakfast on the terrace outside the kitchen/living room. "We should plan a trip to the USA to visit Nathan next year," suggested Jimi.

"Yes, that would be great, I think my mum would love to visit Nathan as well. It could also be her sixtieth birthday celebration. Don't say anything yet, especially to your mum. I want it to be a surprise for her."

After Jimi had eaten his breakfast and was getting ready to leave, Nathan came out from his bedroom. "Uncle Jimi, are you going to leave without saying goodbye?"

Nathan gave Jimi a hug. "Many thanks for everything you have done for us, and for the watch."

"Don't mention it. Besides, when we get old, you're going to take care of me and your old man and push us around in our wheelchairs." They all laughed.

"I'll see you in the USA. I would love to visit you there," Jimi said to Nathan, while hugging him goodbye.

The two of them started packing after Jimi left. "Before going to the airport, I need to buy more chocolates for grandmother," Nathan said, "Mama Evelyn, Olivia and my American host family."

Andrew called back to him from across the room, "Let's see how much space we still have in our suitcases, then let's hit the shops right after they open."

They went shopping and bought Swiss chocolate bars/gift boxes that weren't found outside Switzerland and then headed back to the flat to finish their packing.

Nathan told Andrew he hoped that one day he would find a great, meaningful job like Uncle Jimi had done and be able to afford to live in a place like his.

Andrew nodded, though in Andrew's mind Nathan would be able to do anything and achieve anything. In Andrew's eyes, Nathan was a bright, polite and down-to-earth young man who had a great future in front of him.

Andrew pushed the envelope containing the keys into the far end of the mailbox as a pre-ordered airport pick-up taxi waited for them at the entrance of the building. The taxi driver joked with them about their heavy suitcases. Andrew said, "My son bought a ton of chocolates for all his girlfriends back home." They all laughed.

They arrived home late that afternoon and Andrew stayed in to start working and answering emails. Nathan went straight to the restaurant to give the chocolates to his grandmother and Mama Evelyn. That evening Nathan stayed at Hilary's place.

One early evening, two days after Andrew and Nathan had left Jimi's flat and just a few days before Nathan was to depart for the USA, Andrew got a phone call from Jimi. Jimi sounded very distressed. "My flat has been burgled."

"What! What happened?" Andrew asked, and seemed to be in an even more distressed state than Jimi was.

When Jimi got home Tuesday evening he hadn't been able to find the keys Andrew had put in the envelope, and thought maybe Andrew had forgotten about it. When he got up to his floor, he saw that his door wasn't closed properly. He went in to find that many of his small collectables and jewellery pieces were missing.

Jimi called the police, who came by and called in forensic experts to see if the burglar had left any fingerprints. He had to submit a report to the insurance company, but since there had not been a forced entry, the police weren't too optimistic about it. "Someone must have found the keys inside the mailbox and got in while I was away for those two days," Jimi explained.

"Jimi, I'm so sorry to hear that. Is there anything I can do?" Andrew's stomach turned.

Jimi told Andrew that he and Nathan might have to go to the Consulate General of Switzerland in Edinburgh to make a statement and provide a copy of their passports.

"Of course. Anything." Andrew comforted Jimi and then hung up the phone. He felt awful about the burglary and felt he was responsible for it.

When Nathan came back after visiting Olivia in Glasgow, Andrew told him about the incident; he, too, was badly affected. He immediately sent a text message to Jimi to say how sorry he was about the break-in.

In the evening, Andrew received a text from Jimi.

The bastard stole all my underwear collection.

As he went through the flat, Jimi must have discovered bit-by-bit what had been stolen.

The next day, Andrew received another message from Jimi, informing him of the case number and instructions that he and Nathan needed to go to the Consulate General of Switzerland in Edinburgh, make a declaration and forward a copy of their passports.

Andrew called the Consulate first, but didn't know that he would have to make an appointment; the next possible appointment was Monday of the next week. Thankfully, the lady he spoke to was very understanding, once he had explained to her the urgency of the situation and that Nathan would be leaving for the USA in two days' time, Andrew got an appointment in the morning of the same Friday Nathan and Olivia were due to return to the USA.

They rushed there and made a declaration before heading to the airport, and they were told that the statement would be forwarded to the Swiss police department and the insurance company.

The investigation of the case continued.

Chapter 8
Vole

Life is unpredictable and can be cruel at times. Your whole world can be turned upside down without warning.

That Thursday, as usual, it was bridge night for Hilary and Mama Evelyn. The routine was for Hilary and Mama Evelyn to change before going.

When designing and refurbishing the restaurant for Mama Evelyn, in addition to a shower room for the staff, Mr Walker and Andrew had also installed a bathroom with a bath in the back office of the restaurant, which she really liked. That bathroom was designated for use by Mama Evelyn and Hilary only, and they both valued that extra luxury.

After a long day at work, Hilary needed to take a shower. Mama Evelyn had already changed and was talking to Joey at the front of the restaurant. Joey was considering moving back to Edinburgh permanently from Newcastle, as he was going through a divorce. Mama Evelyn waited for Hilary, but got a bit worried as she hadn't come out of the bathroom; she had been in there for quite some time.

"Hilary, how are you getting on? We have to hurry up." Mama Evelyn knocked on the door lightly at first. When she heard no reply, she knocked again, but this time with force, and she shouted, "Hilary, are you all right?"

When she didn't receive a response from Hilary, she got scared and called for Joey. They managed to open the door and saw Hilary lying on the floor. She must have fainted and hit her head on the edge of the bath. There was blood coming from the back of her head.

Joey quickly called an ambulance and then phoned Andrew. Andrew was in a client meeting and did not pick up the phone. Joey kept calling, and finally left a message for Andrew to call back urgently.

Mama Evelyn and Joey followed the ambulance to the hospital and waited for Andrew. When Andrew finally heard the message and called back, the ambulance had already taken Hilary to the emergency room. By the time Andrew got to the hospital, Hilary had already been declared dead.

"Your mother had a minor stroke, and at the same time her blood pressure and heart rate went down, which caused her to faint and pass out. But her death was actually due to the blow she received to the back of her head on the edge of the bath when she fell. Her heart stopped, and despite our best efforts, we were not able to save her."

Absolutely spinning, Andrew heard the doctor's explanation through a very long and distant tunnel. Andrew raged about having to experience this maelstrom of shock and grief with his mother's death just barely five years after the tragic and untimely death of his son.

A few weeks earlier, Hilary had mentioned to Andrew that she felt light-headed and dizzy. Andrew was extremely alarmed and was upset with Hilary, as she wouldn't go to the doctor and just brushed it off as if it was nothing or that she was just tired.

Andrew was frustrated and upset with himself. 'Why didn't I insist on her going to the doctor? Or just make an appointment for her?' Those questions repeated in his head.

The next few days were a total blur for Andrew, apart from those questions drumming in his head. It was almost like he was just going through the motions. He was in a state of denial and afraid of facing the reality and his true pain. Thankfully, Joey and Mama Evelyn were there to help, contacting the Procurator Fiscal, as the death was caused as the result of an accident, registering with the Registrar of Birth, Deaths and Marriages about the death, contacting the funeral home, arranging for the funeral and informing friends and family about the death and the wake.

When Andrew told Lena and invited her to the service, much to Andrew's surprise, she actually came all the way from Sweden and turned up at the service out of respect for Hilary, knowing that she had practically raised Nathan for her. Lena barely spoke to Andrew during the funeral service, as she didn't want to disturb him. To her, he looked so fragile and disconnected. The way she greeted him was as if she was afraid to burden him with her own sorrows and knew that he would have broken down from words with the slightest emotional attachment.

Mama Evelyn was a rock throughout. With the help of Joey, Sami and Jimi, Mama Evelyn organised Hilary's burial and her funeral service. Andrew wouldn't have been able to handle all the matters and legal requirements that came with the death of his loved one.

For Mama Evelyn, it was keeping as busy as possible that helped her to avoid thinking about her own grief around losing Hilary, her friend for almost thirty-five years. They had supported each other through thick and thin; especially since their husbands were absent for a large part of their married lives, and basically, they had both raised their children single-handedly.

The service was respectful and beautiful, but intense. Andrew had chosen a song called 'Vole', meaning 'Fly' in French, performed by Céline Dion, a song she sang paying tribute to her niece, who lost her battle to cancer. As her voice filled the room — 'Fly, fly, little sister, fly my angel, my pain, leave your body and us so your suffering finally ends…' — in tears, it took Andrew back to his own childhood, growing up without his father. He thought about Nathan, about the joy and pride he brought to Hilary's life and how his death had made a permanent dent in Hilary's heart, which no money in the world or time was able to mend.

At the end of the service a woman approached Andrew. He recognised her. It was Mrs Lloyd. He had met her when Hilary had told Andrew to join when the bridge club came to Mama Evelyn's restaurant for lunch one Sunday.

"Oh, my dear Andrew, I'm so sorry for your loss." She gave Andrew a hug.

"Thank you for coming. I'm so glad that many of her friends turned up for the service."

"Andrew, I'm going to tell you something; although you might think it's a bit strange." She paused and led Andrew aside, and lowered her voice a bit before continuing, "Do you remember Mrs Ford? She used to be part of our bridge club. She is now in a nursing home." Andrew nodded.

"She had a stroke and two minor heart attacks. She survived skin cancer and had to have one of her legs amputated due to her diabetic condition. She has lost her sight and is hard of hearing. All she wants is to die, but this woman is still alive in spite of all her ailments. I think the only thing that will eventually kill her is boredom." Mrs Lloyd made an awkward sound, almost as if to laugh at her own witty remark, but she was quite visibly feeling worried, hopeless and frustrated for Mrs Ford.

Andrew looked at her, not knowing where this conversation was heading.

"What I'm trying to say is that I'm very sad that you have lost your mother and that you didn't have a chance to say goodbye to her. But, at times, living is not everything, and it could be more painful. If I were to end up like Mrs Ford, I, too, would wish I could die suddenly, as your mother did." Mrs Lloyd continued, "Sorry, my son, to load all this on to you, but I've recently been diagnosed with dementia. Forgive an old woman for talking nonsense. But what am I going to do?" She was tearful and sounded lost and frightened.

Other friends of Hilary, wanting to give him hugs and their condolences, pulled Andrew away. But Mrs Lloyd's words about an early and respectful death being preferable to living without dignity stuck in his head. 'I must talk to Mama Evelyn and visit Mrs Ford and Mrs Lloyd one day.'

After the funeral, it seemed everything went back to 'normal' again. For the first years after Hilary's passing, Andrew wasn't able to talk about her, and he was even afraid to dream about her. He just wasn't ready to face his grief.

But, one evening the dreams started.

In one dream, Andrew was supposed to meet up with Hilary. He went to the place where they were expected to meet and was told that she had just left to go to somewhere else. He rushed to the new meeting place and was told the same thing; he had just missed her. This continued until the pain in his chest caused by the sorrow he experienced woke him up.

In another dream, Hilary was looking at him and, for whatever reason, they were unable to communicate. He'd wake up, the pillow wet with his tears. A few times, in a dream he just called out "Mum!" and was woken up by his own shouting.

With time, Andrew dreamt less and less about Hilary and Nathan, but there wasn't a day that went by without him thinking about them. Only one thought made living each day without them more bearable and comforted him, knowing that each day he lived brought him one day closer to the time when he'd meet Hilary and Nathan again — the two most important people in his life. One gave birth to him, and the other he brought into this life.

Chapter 9
Closure

To show his appreciation for her coming all the way from Sweden for Hilary's service, Andrew invited Lena to dinner before she flew back home. Much to Andrew's surprise, she accepted.

Andrew arrived at the restaurant first, sat down and waited for Lena. For a brief moment he regretted arranging to meet up with her on his own. The last time Andrew and Lena had met was at Nathan's funeral service after Andrew had returned from the USA with his ashes, which was almost four years ago. Intentionally or unintentionally, they'd had very little to do with each other since Nathan's death, but Andrew had learned that Lena and his mum had still kept in regular contact.

'What am I going to say to her? What are we going to talk about?' Andrew was lost in his own thoughts.

At the same moment, Lena arrived. She didn't feel comfortable being the first to arrive, so she was hoping Andrew was already there. Luckily, as she looked inside the restaurant from the window, she saw him. He didn't see her at first.

'He seems to be miles away with his own thoughts. Oh, Andrew, you look so vulnerable and lost!'

All she wanted to do at that point was to go up to the table and comfort Andrew with a hug, but at the same time Lena questioned her acceptance of the dinner invitation alone with him. She felt so sorry for him, she wasn't sure if she would be able to cope with his emotional state.

Suddenly, Andrew looked up and saw Lena through the window. Seeing him looking at her, without any hesitation she opened the door and entered the restaurant. He stood up and waved. The waiter accompanied her to his table. The pair hugged awkwardly and, at first, they were overly polite, as if they were afraid to discuss anything that might upset each other. Throughout the meal they had a kind of ping-pong conversation about the weather, the menu and the decor of the restaurant. Andrew thanked Lena for coming all that way to attend the service; Lena commented on how beautiful the service was and how many of Hilary's friends had turned up.

They both jumped slightly when, lying on the table, Lena's mobile phone vibrated and rang, increasing in volume. The screen lit up. Lena had Nathan's photo as her screen-saver; one of the last pictures taken of Nathan, dressed in his dinner jacket at Lena's wedding, outside the church. Nathan was the only tie between these two otherwise strangers, and the only reason they had been brought together to sit and have dinner.

Afraid of making eye contact, they both stared at the image of Nathan for a few brief seconds, till Lena harshly disconnected the call after she realised who the caller was. "It's Leif. I'll call him back." There was a moment of silence; then, without being able to control her emotions, she burst into tears.

Attempting to comfort her, Andrew placed his hand over her hand that was resting on the table. Though it had been almost four years since Nathan's death, the thought of talking about him was still too raw for either of them. They stayed silent and both felt awkward, as if they didn't know how to handle the situation because they had never really talked about the struggle of loss they had faced, nor how they had felt about Nathan's death.

Finally, Lena looked into Andrew's eyes and broke the silence. "Was I a bad mother? Was it my fault to send him to the USA? Was it my fault agreeing to buy him a car?" Lena asked earnestly.

"How could you even think that?" Andrew said, struggling to hold back his tears as well, especially when he recognised all too well the niggling self-doubt and self-blame.

"I left Nathan with you and your mother and went back to Sweden. I was too young and didn't even know what I was supposed to do with my life, let alone be a mother and take care of a baby. I was depressed and wasn't coping well with the situation I was in." She cried in silence.

"When he was little, I wanted to take him back to Sweden with me, but when I saw the bond between him and your mother, I just didn't have the heart to do that to both of them. Oh, God! I miss him so much."

"Lena, you were such a good mother to Nathan. We were both so young when he first came into our lives. He came to us as a gift; a gift we had for nineteen years and will cherish for the rest of our lives. From the bottom of my heart I thank you for letting Nathan stay in Edinburgh. It meant a lot to my mother."

Lena smiled shyly at Andrew.

"Leif and I were in Vienna last year and we visited the Sisi Museum — a museum dedicated to the Empress Elisabeth of Austria. In one of the descriptions about her life I learned that in 1898 her son died at thirty when she was about fifty. The effects of the death of her son were so profound and far-reaching, she withdrew from public life and court duties. She drowned in her sorrows and never really recovered..." Lena now looked deeply into Andrew's eyes.

"Are you okay?" Andrew interrupted, to make sure she was not in too much pain.

Lena nodded gently. "But I had nowhere to go and nowhere to hide. I had to consider the feelings and pain of my children losing their brother and my parents losing their first grandson. I still had to be a mother, a wife and a daughter. I felt I owed it to them and needed to be strong for them. I still went to work and still ate and drank; as stupid as it sounds, I still got frustrated about heavy traffic when driving." She took a sip of wine. "What is wrong with me? How was I able to continue living after my son died?"

"Lena, don't be so hard on yourself. We all need time to grieve and process our pain in the only way we know how. I've asked myself the same questions. How am I still coping with daily routines? How come the world didn't just stop? How come I still have a desire for anything?"

Andrew had never felt so close to Lena as in this moment. He was able to relate to her pain; the way she had to forego her own grief like he had done, because he had been afraid to burden his mother with his own.

After a few moments of silence, they both calmed down and started to enjoy each other's company. They ordered another bottle of wine. They laughed about the first time they had met and how panicked Lena was when she found out she was pregnant with Nathan at only eighteen years old. They also shared and laughed about some funny stories and incidents about Nathan and his quirky habits. They then laughed hard about silly jokes. They knew they needed this occasion to be happy for Nathan's sake and they also realised that it might be the last time they would ever see each other.

After dinner, Andrew walked Lena back to her hotel. As they were saying goodbye, Lena gave Andrew a heartfelt hug. "Andrew, if I haven't said it before, I would like to thank you for arranging Nathan's cremation and bringing him back to Edinburgh. I went to Nathan's grave this morning and can't thank you and your mother enough for looking after it and keeping it so nice." She looked tenderly at Andrew.

"My mother and I couldn't have been more grateful to you for letting us bury Nathan's ashes here in Edinburgh. It meant a lot to us, especially to my mother. I know she visited Nathan's grave at least once a week before her passing. Caring for his grave gave her a purpose; it was something she was still able to do for her grandson and somewhere she was able to go to be near him." Andrew continued in an assured tone, "I will look after Nathan's grave."

"I wouldn't have it any other way. I know how much Nathan meant to your mother. I had a lot of respect and admiration for her. She was really a wonderful grandmother to Nathan. They had a very special bond." Lena held Andrew's hand firmly.

"You know, I never want to fully process my grief over the loss of Nathan as I'm afraid I will miss him less." Andrew held Lena's hand firmly for a few seconds, letting her know it was a sign of his respect, appreciation and understanding towards her.

"Oh, Andrew. I'm the same. I don't ever want to get over it. Thank you for bringing Nathan into our lives."

"Well, as if I were able to do it by myself without your help."

They both chuckled and could see the tears running down each other's faces.

Andrew waved goodbye. "Regards to Leif and the kids, and have a safe journey back home."

"Take good care of yourself."

As Lena wiped away her tears and waved goodbye, the light from the hotel entrance reflected on her blonde hair and face, and for a split-second Andrew saw Nathan in her smile. For that brief moment, he sensed Nathan's presence.

Lena went into the hotel and Andrew walked home. They had parted. Maybe this time it was for good.

Chapter 10
Dreams of a Wedding

Before Hilary's funeral service, Andrew spoke several times with Aunt Betty over the phone. Once, he called her using Hilary's Skype account from Hilary's laptop, just like Hilary and Betty used to do before Hilary died.

Andrew was taken aback by how much Betty resembled his mother. Although they were identical twins, Aunt Betty had put on a few extra pounds and her hair was a different style and colour, but Andrew was devastated when he saw his mother's double on the computer screen for the first time since Hilary's death. From the way Aunt Betty talked and expressed herself, it was like seeing and talking to his mum again.

"Andrew, I hope you don't mind me telling you, but more than once your mum told me that she had three great sorrows in her life. First was your father had left when you were still very little; the second was you are not in a relationship; and the thing that broke her heart more than anything was Nathan's death."

Aunt Betty also told Andrew that Hilary's biggest dream and joy would have been to attend Nathan's wedding. When she told him that, Andrew wasn't able to restrain himself any longer; he just sobbed uncontrollably.

When he stopped, Aunt Betty said jokingly, "May I share with you a secret about your mother?" She sounded playful and excited. "I don't know when she started, but before Nathan's death your mother already bought a few hats in advance for his wedding in the future, and she even modelled them for me via Skype." They both burst out laughing.

After Hilary died, Andrew avoided it for as long as he could, but he knew he had to clear up his mother's flat. This was the place where he grew up and where Nathan grew up, before they moved to their current home.

A few days after the funeral service, Andrew entered the flat and there was a strong damp smell and piles of post on the floor of the entrance. The last time Andrew had needed to go there was a few days before the burial with Mama Evelyn; she was there with him to choose clothes for Hilary to be dressed.

This time he was there by himself, and it felt a bit odd and surreal, looking around... the living room, the kitchen, her bedroom and his old bedroom, which he hadn't been in for years. Andrew hadn't been inside that room since he and Nathan had moved out. Nathan hadn't been in that room either for a few years. Andrew couldn't remember when it started, but when Nathan came over to stay at his grandmother's place, she would let him sleep in her bed and she would sleep in the living room. "It's too messy," she used to say.

For some reason, Andrew was a bit nervous about opening the door of his old bedroom. But when he did, he made a shocking discovery.

The room was full of hats, more than a hundred of them; some of them inside their original boxes piled on the bed, some of them inside the cupboard, some of them packed in plastic bags pinned on the wall, and some of them packed in plastic bags on the floor. They were of various sizes, shapes, designs, colours, materials, styles, and accessories, but all with one thing in common, they were all to be worn at a festive event — a wedding. Inside the cupboard he also found boxes of baby clothes, shoes, toys and drawings that used to belong to Nathan. 'I thought we had already given them away to friends or to charity shops years ago.'

Andrew was stunned by the vast collection and didn't know what to do with all those hats. He called Mama Evelyn to come over and witness this extraordinary find.

After Mama Evelyn arrived, they sat on the floor, quietly thinking about how Hilary must have dreamt of Nathan's wedding and her choice of outfit. They had no idea when Hilary had started to buy all these hats. Hilary had always been careful with money, so it was even more surprising to Evelyn and Andrew, as she must have spent a fortune on them and continued with her collection even after Nathan's death. Maybe it was a way to escape the pain of losing Nathan.

"What should we do with all these hats?" From her look, Andrew knew Mama Evelyn wasn't keen on the idea of giving them all to charity shops.

"Who would want them?" Andrew asked, sounding a bit deflated and exhausted.

Mama Evelyn thought long and hard. "What about giving some to the ladies in the church and the bridge club which your mum and I belong to?" She continued, "You know, after Nathan's death, the bridge club was a place she was able to escape to, even just for a few hours a week for her to forget." Andrew nodded, as he had no idea what to do with them.

"I will ask Joey to come and help you to lift all these boxes," said Mama Evelyn.

"Oh, thanks. I am glad Joey has definitely moved back here from Newcastle." Andrew carefully avoided mentioning Joey's, as yet not finalised, messy divorce and the custody battle with his wife over their two sons.

Mama Evelyn left after she had helped to sort the hats into different piles; some to give away to the ladies in the church and the bridge club and some to donate to charity shops. Andrew started packing all the hats into boxes and thought to himself that he would like to keep a few as a memory of his mother. Looking around, there were two hats, stacked together, that he was drawn to, so he put them aside.

When all the hats were sorted into boxes, Andrew remembered the two he had put aside. He picked them up and wanted to look at them individually. As they were stacked on top of each other, he went to separate them and something dropped out. It was an envelope.

Andrew recognised the handwriting on it. It was from Nathan to his grandmother. From the date on the stamp, it was sent before the Christmas just before Nathan had died in a car accident.

'It must be the last letter he sent her,' he thought.

Holding the envelope in his hands, Andrew's heart was beating rapidly and his hands were trembling. He opened the envelope carefully, trying to control his anticipation. Inside, he found a card and a US 100 dollar note.

Dear Nan,
    Merry Christmas and Happy New Year.

It was great talking to you the other day. I know you were disappointed that I am not coming home for Christmas. I promise to come home next summer, or you and dad can come and visit me.

I have found a part-time job delivering Chinese takeout. They were impressed that I was able to speak and understand words in Cantonese. ☺ Please let Mama Evelyn know and say hello for me.

The $100 bill is the first wage I received and I would like you to have it.

I promise to always drive carefully and slowly.
Love,
Nathan

Tears ran down his face. Andrew now remembered that his mum had told him about the 100-dollar note that Nathan had sent her. Even though it was a few years ago, Andrew still vividly recalled the image of his mum proudly waving the card and the 100-dollar note in the air and telling Andrew, "I will cherish it forever and will never spend it."

He carefully folded the money and held it close to his heart. Andrew had never felt as close to his mum and to Nathan as he did at that moment. 'This will stay with me till the day I die.'

Chapter 11
Step by Step I Am Falling
Part I

As Andrew was making the bed for Justin, he started having doubts about Justin's visit. He thought, 'What will we talk about and what on earth do we have in common?' He was not sure how he felt about the hug he had received from Justin, which made him wonder if inviting Justin to stay was such a good idea after all.

Andrew almost wanted to call Jimi and tell him about Justin's visit, but wasn't sure what to say. He managed to convince himself not to dwell on it further and to get on with the dinner. He loved cooking and preparing meals for company. He found it much more fun to cook for others rather than just for himself. Normally, he didn't even bother.

The menu would be sliced tomatoes and mozzarella cheese, and to make it more professional-looking he decorated it with fresh Italian basil leaves. He would drizzle balsamic vinegar and olive oil just before serving. For the main course, Andrew prepared chicken parmesan, a dish he learned many years ago when he'd travelled to Italy for a cookery class, and which was Nathan's favourite. For dessert, Andrew made a Swedish chocolate cake.

As he was stirring the tomato sauce for the main course, the buzzer rang. 'Is it already that time?' He checked the clock on the oven, then pressed the button to unlock the downstairs' entrance, and a few minutes later Justin's smiley face appeared as he opened the flat door.

"Hi, Mr Hughes, it is great to see you again," said Justin, and he handed over a box of chocolates and a bottle of wine.

"Come in! You didn't need to bring anything. That's very kind of you." Andrew closed the door and took the chocolates and the bottle of wine so Justin was able to take off his jacket and shoes as he entered the flat. "Let me show you where you are going to sleep tonight. You can put your bag down in there."

It was Nathan's room, which Andrew had renovated and refurbished a few years ago and turned into a guest room.

"Wow! What a nice place you have," Justin said, as he looked around the room and put down his bag.

"I hope you can sleep well tonight. Let me show you the rest of the flat. Hope you are hungry."

"I'm always hungry." They both laughed.

They really enjoyed dinner, and Justin complimented Andrew's cooking many times. He was particularly impressed with the Swedish chocolate cake, of which he had three helpings.

"So, what are you doing in Edinburgh?" Andrew asked.

Justin explained the reason for his visit. He had made an appointment to talk to an advisor at Edinburgh University to see whether it would be possible for him to transfer his last year's Master's degree studies to Edinburgh. Justin also talked excitedly about Rebecca, his fiancée, and the plans for their upcoming wedding in two years and their future together. Then, out of the blue, he said that he and Rebecca had a lot of gay friends and asked about whether Andrew had a boyfriend.

Trying not to show how uncomfortable he was with the topic and his question, Andrew told him that there wasn't much to tell, as he'd been single for quite a while now. The unspoken meaning was that Andrew didn't want to talk about his personal life, especially to Justin, whom he didn't know well enough.

Finally, and inevitably, Justin also talked about Nathan — another landmine topic for Andrew, which made him even more uncomfortable. Andrew wasn't sure whether it was the alcohol or whether his anxiety and fatigue had kicked in, or the subject about his relationship status and about Nathan, but suddenly he felt a strong need to be alone. He looked at his watch, it was only a bit after ten p.m.

Without realising it, Andrew yawned. He looked slightly embarrassed and said apologetically to Justin, "I really enjoyed spending time catching up after so many years since we first met, but I feel a bit tired, so would you mind if we call it a night?"

Justin seemed visibly hurt and surprised. "Did I say something wrong?" he asked cautiously.

"Not at all. I'm just a bit tired, and maybe I've drunk too much, too fast. I'll make you breakfast tomorrow morning and after your meeting with the university, come back here for lunch. I have to do a bit of work tomorrow, but would be more than happy to show you around Edinburgh." Andrew continued, "Please stay up and watch TV if you want, and there is more wine; make yourself at home."

Andrew showed Justin where to find towels and said good night. He took a shower, then went to bed. He had a very unsettling night, because he dreamt about Nathan, his mother and oddly his father, whom he hadn't thought of for years. He was woken up by his iPhone alarm set for eight a.m. He stretched and sat up in bed; then he suddenly remembered he had a visitor in the guest room. He got up and took a quick shower and went to the kitchen to make breakfast.

Justin was up as well and already dressed. He came into the kitchen and said, "Thanks for the dinner, Mr Hughes. I'm leaving now."

Andrew was surprised. "Why? Don't you want any breakfast?"

"It's okay. I usually don't eat much in the morning. I'll just walk to the university from here and have a cup of coffee when I get there."

'He sounds a bit distant and overly polite,' Andrew thought, but couldn't grasp why.

"Are you sure? So, shall I see you after your appointment? I'll prepare some lunch for us, and in the afternoon I will take time off from work and I can show you Edinburgh." Andrew was still trying to change Justin's mind.

"Oh, I'm not sure. I'll see how the appointment goes."

"Please do come back. I will make us something nice for lunch."

"Bye, Mr Hughes. Thanks again for having me last night."

Andrew thought he seemed to have convinced Justin to come back for lunch, as he looked less frosty when he said goodbye. It was only 8.25 a.m.

Andrew had a quick breakfast and started working, but felt a bit unsettled about the way Justin had left.

Around ten-fifteen a.m., a message came from Justin.

Mr Hughes, the meeting went well and I'm heading to the bus station now. Thanks for the kind offer, but I won't come by for lunch. Thanks again for last night. Justin.

At first, Andrew was quite frustrated, as he didn't know what he had done wrong or how he had offended Justin. He counted to ten and took a deep breath and then replied,

Hi, Justin, glad to know the meeting went well. I'm really puzzled why you suddenly wanted to go back to Glasgow. I am really sorry if I offended you in any way. That wasn't my intention. I enjoyed talking to you and hope to see you soon. The next time you come, I'll take you to see Nathan's grave. Take good care of yourself. Andrew.

For the rest of the day, Andrew was swamped with work and visited a few flats for sale that had recently been advertised.

11.05 p.m., a message came in.

Good evening, Mr Hughes. Sorry about my abrupt departure today. I wasn't myself last night and this morning. I thought that I was the one who offended you with my question about your private life, and if I did, I'm sorry. I didn't mean anything by it. I would

very much like to visit you again. If you are available, I can come down next weekend. Justin.

Andrew was already half asleep, so he only read the whole message the next morning and replied,

Great. Come by Friday evening after six and you can stay the whole weekend if you want. Andrew.

A few minutes later, a message came from Justin.

Will be in touch once I have purchased my tickets. Justin. ☺

In the afternoon, Andrew couldn't stand the suspense any longer, so he called Jimi in Spain and told him about Justin's first visit and about his upcoming visit next weekend.

A few years ago, the Red Cross, where Jimi's partner Vincent worked, had asked him to relocate. Jimi and Vincent had a long discussion about it and in the end they both handed in their notices and sold their flats in Geneva and in Lausanne. They moved to a small holiday resort outside Alicante, Spain, and now operated an upscale and exclusive gay B&B. They had both made quite a handsome profit in the move, so they were able to buy a huge house in Spain after the economic crash in the real estate market in 2008.

"Do you know why you want to see him again?" Jimi shared his scepticism, as he wasn't so keen on the idea.

"I don't know, but I just thought it would be nice to show him Edinburgh. There's nothing to be worried about, as he has a fiancée and they are getting married in two years." Somehow Andrew didn't know why he felt like he needed to justify his actions.

"Really, be careful, Andrew. I don't want to see you getting hurt." Jimi sounded a bit worried.

For a brief moment, Andrew felt somewhat defensive and didn't want to talk any more about wanting to see Justin again, so he quickly changed the subject.

"Thanks. And what about yours and Vincent's idea of having a baby through surrogacy, now that a ban has been imposed in Thailand?"

"We can do it in other countries, but it's either too expensive or legally too messy, with too many uncertainties." Jimi sighed.

No wonder Jimi sounded a bit disappointed, as having a child was the biggest dream of his life.

"Well, Uncle Jimi, you can always adopt me or just include me in your will. You know I don't eat much and I don't need nappies any more." Andrew tried to cheer him up.

"Yes, I'll include you in my will and leave you all my used and worn-out underwear."

They both chuckled.

After they hung up, Andrew was still convinced that Jimi was worrying for nothing.

The following days passed by very quickly. During the week, Andrew exchanged a few brief text messages with Justin to confirm his arrival on Friday. For some reason, Andrew was hardly able to concentrate on work; he was really looking forward to Friday evening and the weekend.

The weather was terrible on Friday, so Andrew was a bit worried that Justin might want to cancel; but around six p.m. he showed up, dripping wet; it was pouring outside. Andrew welcomed Justin in and told him to take a warm shower straight away and get changed so he wouldn't catch a cold.

While Justin was in the shower, Andrew was in the kitchen preparing dinner. Andrew also made a cup of hot ginger tea for Justin — one of the many home remedies he had learned from Mama Evelyn.

"Here. Drink this, so you won't catch a cold." Andrew handed the cup of hot ginger tea to Justin.

Later, over dinner, they had a really good time talking and laughing. Andrew turned on the fire and they sat together on the sofa watching TV. Andrew poured them both a whisky; the atmosphere was calm and pleasant.

Suddenly, Justin turned his back towards Andrew and asked him whether it would be okay if Andrew gave him a back massage. Andrew was quite stunned by this request, but his hands pre-empted his rational thoughts. He started to massage Justin's head, shoulder and back. A while later, Andrew asked him to lie down on the sofa so Andrew could massage his feet and legs. From his facial and body expressions, Andrew could tell that Justin was enjoying it, making Andrew even more eager to please him. God knows, Andrew was enjoying it, too.

Andrew massaged Justin with deeper hand pressure, and as Andrew was about to massage Justin's thighs, he stood up and without warning said in a frosty voice, "Mr Hughes, sorry, but I don't want to continue." He then walked in to the bathroom.

While waiting for him to come back, Andrew felt such an idiot. 'What was I thinking? What was I expecting?' If there had been a hole in the ground, he would have jumped right into it.

After a while, Justin came out of the bathroom and popped his head into the living room. "Mr Hughes, I'm a bit tired, so I'm going to bed now. Thanks for a lovely dinner tonight. See you tomorrow morning." He said it abruptly as he headed to his room.

"Good night, see you tomorrow." Andrew must have controlled his voice, not sounding too embarrassed and confused about what had just happened.

His first thought was to contact Jimi, but then he realised that would be really humiliating. It goes without saying, he had a sleepless night. When the next morning arrived, Justin was himself again, which was much to Andrew's relief.

They had brunch and both went back to bed again as the rain still hadn't stopped and, worse yet, there were now strong winds. When they finally woke up in the afternoon, they talked about visiting Nathan's grave, but the weather had worsened, so they decided to stay in and just watch TV and relax.

Andrew told Justin that he was sorry that they hadn't gone out today, as he had promised to show him Edinburgh.

"Don't worry about it. I enjoy just having a relaxing and lazy weekend."

Justin then told Andrew that he had just Skyped with Rebecca and she had said to say hello.

"Oh, thanks. Please send her my regards the next time you speak to her."

Luckily, Andrew had bought enough food, so he prepared a nice dinner for them both. He cooked Thai green curry with chicken and was happily surprised how much Justin enjoyed the spicy food.

After last night's episode, Andrew was very uneasy about how he should act; he sat rigidly on the sofa after dinner while they watched TV. The rain really was non-stop and it felt ten times worse with the strong winds. History was repeating itself; the TV was on, the fire was on and, whiskies in hand, Andrew heard Justin whisper, "Mr Hughes, I would like to reciprocate the massage you gave me last night. Is that okay?"

"Are you sure? You don't need to do that." Andrew was really not sure about this, and tried not to sound too excited.

"I want to, though I might not be as good as you." He smiled a shy smile and had already turned round to Andrew's back and started to massage him.

Andrew closed his eyes and really enjoyed Justin's hands slowly running over his head, face, back and shoulders. Justin took Andrew's arms and stretched them out and pressed his chest against Andrew's back. Justin's head was very close and Andrew could feel Justin's warm breath behind his ear.

Andrew was enjoying it so much he felt his body and mind completely relax, but with a feeling of euphoria. It seemed as though the massage lasted for a lifetime but, in reality, it was only a few minutes. At one point, Andrew felt Justin's lips brush lightly past his neck. His body stiffened, but he thought to himself that must have been an accident, so he relaxed again. Suddenly, Justin lightly kissed Andrew's neck and although it was but a brief second, Andrew felt it.

'Holy Moly, I am going to hell,' Andrew said to himself.

At this point, Justin was behind Andrew, and he felt some parts of their bodies were getting too close, but he didn't have the willpower to stop it; nor did he want to. Justin slowed down, but still had his arms around Andrew. Andrew turned around and hugged Justin and moved his arms up and down Justin's back. Andrew kissed Justin's neck, but when he went to kiss him on the lips, Justin turned his head away while still holding Andrew.

"Mr Hughes, I can't. I love Rebecca and wouldn't do anything to hurt her. I enjoy spending time with you, but wouldn't want to lead you on."

Once again Andrew felt confused, deflated and frustrated. 'What am I supposed to say? I've never felt so intimate with someone like this before, and how could this wrong feel so right. And... why are we still holding each other?' These thoughts ran through his head.

Andrew rested his head on Justin's shoulder and they were both silent. The TV was on low and they just stayed in each other's arms for a while, before going to their separate bedrooms for the night.

The next morning, as Andrew opened the door and was about to come out from the bathroom, he saw Justin was approaching it. "Oh, good morning. Hope you slept well," Andrew said awkwardly.

"Morning. Thanks. May I use the bathroom?"

"Of course."

Andrew made room for Justin to enter as he walked out. Both avoided eye contact throughout this short encounter outside the bathroom.

Andrew prepared brunch for them both and after they ate the tension and the awkwardness seemed to have melted and they were both talking normally again to each other.

"It looks like the weather will not change for the better. Maybe we shouldn't go to the grave today. Hope it is okay with you?"

Justin seemed a bit disappointed, but agreed that the rain and wind were not ideal to visit the graveyard.

"Welcome to Scotland," Andrew joked about the Scottish weather to lighten up the mood.

They spent the whole weekend enjoying each other's company and they didn't go out once. Andrew just enjoyed taking care of Justin and spending time with him. For the first time since Nathan's death, Andrew actually felt he was needed. Although he was confused with Justin's on-and-off, ambiguous affection towards him that drove him mad, he still felt alive and was simply happy, as he was doing something for someone and with someone.

The next day, Justin had to go back to Glasgow. He had to finalise a course report and turn it in on Monday, the next day. As Justin was leaving, Andrew handed him a doggy bag with a sandwich and snacks and drinks. "Here. You can have it on the bus."

"Thank you, Mr Hughes. You are spoiling me; you already cooked me a large brunch."

Andrew could see that Justin was really touched by his thoughtfulness. "Oh, wait, I'll get something." Andrew went to his bedroom and came back with a bag from the House of Fraser and handed it to him.

"What is it?" asked Justin with excitement.

He opened the bag and found a wool winter jacket. "Oh, Mr Hughes, you didn't have to buy me anything."

At this point Andrew wasn't sure if Justin liked it, so he said, "I went to the department store the other day and thought that you might look good in this. Come on, try it and see if it fits." Andrew took out the jacket from the bag and handed it to Justin.

Justin put it on and he looked sharp; his blue eyes matched the dark blue colour of the jacket. "I don't know what to say. Thanks, Mr Hughes." He didn't take it off; rather, he put his own jacket in his small travel bag.

Justin and Andrew were both very quiet as they walked to the bus stop. It was raining and they didn't have an umbrella, but they didn't seem to care. As the bus was approaching the stop, Justin looked at Andrew. "Mr Hughes, many thanks for the weekend and the jacket. I really enjoyed spending time with you."

As he was getting on the bus, Andrew said to him, "Send me a message that you got home okay."

"Sure thing." Justin waved as the bus departed.

While Andrew was walking home, his phone rang. Andrew thought it must be Justin, but from the screen he could see it was Mama Evelyn. He could actually hear her warm voice even without speaking to her.

"Good afternoon, Mama Evelyn, how are you?" Andrew answered, at the same time he stopped walking and took shelter in a building's entrance to avoid the rain.

"Andrew, you haven't visited Mama Evelyn for such a long time. Come over for dinner one evening. Sami is getting married in less than three months' time in Hong Kong and we are all going to attend the wedding. You're also her brother, so you must come," said Mama Evelyn in one breath.

"Congratulations! I'm so happy for Sami and, of course, for your family as well. I haven't been in contact with Sami for a while. I would love to go to the wedding and visit Hong Kong. I'll stop by the restaurant next Saturday for dinner and you can tell me more about it." At the same time, Andrew was thinking, 'Should I bring Justin to meet Mama Evelyn as well?'

"Good. I thought you'd forgotten us," said Mama Evelyn. "Jimi and Vincent will fly from Alicante and Joey and I will fly from here. The restaurant will be closed for six weeks." Suddenly, her voice got a bit sentimental. "Andrew, don't be a stranger, come to see Mama Evelyn. I'll prepare you something nice to eat."

"Mama Evelyn, of course I'd love to see you. How could I have forgotten you! It's just that I've been so busy with work lately. So, see you on Saturday, around six p.m. Be good till then... don't do anything I wouldn't approve of!"

Mama Evelyn giggled.

"Okay, okay. Don't forget!" she reminded him once again before she hung up.

When Andrew got home, he really had to restrain himself from contacting Jimi or Olivia about Justin. 'What could I or should I say to them? I am not twenty, thirty or forty; I am approaching fifty. Do I even know what I am getting myself in to? What will all this lead to? What would people say? Is it wrong to feel happy?'

All these questions filled Andrew's head before he fell asleep that night.

On Monday a new client, a referral from one of his previous clients, made contact. This client had bought a penthouse flat in the West End near where Andrew lived and wanted Andrew to do the interior design for it. Andrew recognised the address of the property right away and agreed to meet with the soon-to-be-owners on Friday, when the exchange would take place and when they would get the keys to the property.

During the week, Andrew was busy with other projects and was also looking for buy-to-let properties for other clients.

On Wednesday evening, he received a message from Olivia asking when they were going to meet up. Andrew suggested a few possible dates and agreed in the end that Olivia and her husband should come for dinner on Saturday in two weeks. He hadn't seen Olivia since the welcome party she organised for Justin. 'Am I trying to avoid seeing Olivia?' he wondered.

Andrew also contacted Justin and agreed that he'd come over for the weekend again. They both hoped for better weather so they could visit Nathan's grave.

Oh, I would like to introduce you to Mama Evelyn, a woman very important to me and to Nathan. We are going to have dinner in the restaurant on Saturday. See you Friday around six-thirty p.m.

Andrew sent the message to Justin, but still felt a bit undecided about whether it was a good idea to introduce Justin to Mama Evelyn. At the same time, there was a part of Andrew that wanted to scream out to the whole world and for everyone to see him and Justin together.

On Friday, Andrew met with the new owners at the entrance to the building and visited the penthouse. It was a stunning place with a panoramic view; there weren't any buildings in front of it, either. Andrew was able to see the castle clearly from the living room. The flat had three bedrooms, one of which was en-suite, and there was one extra bathroom at the end of the corridor. The kitchen was huge, with an island in the middle as a breakfast bar. But the whole flat needed to be repainted, and the flooring and bathrooms needed to be refitted.

Andrew took some pictures and promised to work on it over the weekend so as to present a quotation on Tuesday for his work, and the work of any tradesmen used. When he got home in the late afternoon, he started preparing dinner for Justin and himself. He made the bed and put an extra blanket on it for Justin, as it was getting colder.

6.40 p.m., and still no sign of Justin. He tried to convince himself, 'I guess the bus must be late or he took a later bus.'

At 6.55 p.m., Andrew started to get worried, as they had agreed to meet around six-thirty p.m., and Justin was usually on time.

He wanted to call, but then realised he didn't have Justin's mobile number, so he tried phoning through Messenger and it showed that Justin was not connected. By then, Andrew was starting to get really worried. He then sent a Messenger message to Justin, hoping that he might pick it up.

At 7.10 p.m., Andrew was considering calling Olivia, thinking maybe she knew something about what might have happened; but he wasn't sure if it was a good idea. He wasn't sure whether she knew about Justin coming to Edinburgh and spending the weekend with him.

Andrew made himself a stiff gin and tonic, as he needed something to calm his nerves. At 7.25 p.m., Andrew started checking the website for the buses to see whether there were any road accidents.

Suddenly, he caught sight of a picture of Nathan on his desk. The picture had always been there, but this time it felt like Nathan was almost looking back at him. He felt a bit uncomfortable. He closed his eyes and prayed in front of the picture. 'Nathan, please don't let anything happen to Justin. Please, don't let anything happen to him. If seeing him is wrong, I will stop, as long as he is all right.' When Andrew opened his eyes, he looked deeply into Nathan's eyes and said, 'Please, please keep him safe.'

At 7.50 p.m., the bell rang. Andrew jumped and almost ran to press the button to open the door. A few minutes later, Justin's face appeared, and as soon as he was in and the door was closed, Andrew just pulled him in and hugged him really hard; he was so relieved that nothing had happened to him.

"Mr Hughes, so sorry I'm late. You won't believe what happened. I got a special weekend deal, so I rented a car and drove it here." Justin stopped to catch his breath. "I was so psyched to be driving on the wrong side of the road, but then I got a flat tyre on the way and had to stop to change it. Another driver, seeing I was in trouble, was kind enough to help me. I didn't tell you about the car as I wanted it to be a surprise."

In Andrew's head he thought, "How could I be mad at him?' Without saying a word, they just hugged each other tightly for a while. They needed a moment to compose themselves.

Later, as they sat down for dinner, Andrew asked, "I just realised today I don't even have your mobile number — and how come you weren't connected to the internet?"

"I didn't bring my smartphone. I only bought a cheap phone when I got here, with the cheapest contract. I'm able to use Skype, Facebook and Messenger with my laptop." Justin showed him his out-of-date mobile phone.

"Now it makes sense. In that case, can I have your mobile number?"

Andrew pulled out his iPhone and started dialling as Justin said his phone number. "Great, now there is a missed call on your phone and you can see my number as well." Andrew suddenly thought of something. "Wait!" He stood up and went to his office and returned with a smartphone and handed it to Justin. "Here!"

"Mr Hughes, I can't accept this." Justin pushed the phone back to Andrew's side of the table.

"It's okay. I recently bought a new one for work, and if you don't mind using an old phone, you can have it." Andrew didn't think it was a big deal.

"No, it's too much, I can't accept this." Justin really wasn't comfortable accepting it.

"Okay, if it makes you feel any better, you can pay for it. What about a £1?" Andrew smiled.

"No, I can't just pay a £1 for it." Justin thought this was crazy.

Finally, they settled for £20.

"Please remember to reset and erase all the data I have on it. I don't think I have any inappropriate photos or anything in the phone, but I just want to make sure it is clean." Andrew smiled and blushed for no reason. Justin gave Andrew a cheeky look.

After dinner, Justin helped Andrew clear the table and do the dishes, and then Justin sat in the living room and played with the phone he had just bought from Andrew. Andrew entered the living room and poured two glasses of whisky and handed one to Justin. They sat and watched TV; Andrew gently resting his head on Justin's shoulder. There was no need for any words.

The next morning, they woke up late to find the sun was shining. "What a great day," said Andrew, who was in the kitchen preparing brunch, as Justin was heading to the bathroom.

"Good morning, Mr Hughes. Sorry I'm late. I was playing with the phone till late last night."

"Don't worry about it. Take your time. We are not in any kind of hurry," said Andrew, while he sipped his morning coffee.

After his shower, Justin shouted from the bedroom, "I have a car, so I'll drive us there."

Andrew made them both a large brunch. Justin said, "Mr Hughes, you're a really good chef; you cook with your heart." Andrew vaguely recalled someone saying that to him before. He smiled and piled more pancakes onto Justin's plate, like a parent who shows love to their children through food.

They stopped first for some flowers and then drove to the cemetery. As they walked towards Nathan's grave where his ashes were buried, they were both a little anxious and nervous. In front of the grave, Andrew knelt down to place the flowers next to the tombstone. To his surprise, he heard Justin, who was standing right behind him, sobbing quietly. "I'll leave you alone with Nathan for a moment. Take your time."

Andrew didn't look at Justin, but stood up and walked away. He looked on from a distance. He had tears in his eyes as he watched Justin's emotional outpourings at the foot of Nathan's grave.

After Justin composed himself, they sat on a nearby bench. It was the first time Andrew heard about Justin's pain over Nathan's car crash.

"I was supposed to drive them to the university that day for an interview as part of the application for a scholarship. But the day before we had a small argument, and I don't even remember what it was about. I woke up late and Nathan and Olivia had already left. I blamed myself for the car crash, which led to Nathan's death and Olivia's injuries."

Justin continued after a brief pause, "After Nathan's death, it was like everything stopped for me. I didn't care. I dropped out of college and did stupid things. I was self-destructive for a few years, as I hated myself so much. I should have driven them there; or, if there was going to be an accident, I was the one who should have died."

Andrew could see and feel Justin was in real pain. "Justin, don't blame yourself for something you didn't have any control over. Nathan was lucky to have met you, and you two became good friends. You took care of him during the last period of his life, and I am forever thankful for that." Andrew put an arm around Justin's back, to provide him with some comfort.

"My parents didn't know what to do with me, and I didn't know what to do with myself, either. For a long period of time I was in a dark place and thought of committing suicide. It was silly." Justin looked up at the sky and was quiet for a few minutes. "I had nightmares about seeing a rope hanging down, and at the end there was a circle. Many times I imagined myself putting my neck through the rope, and it went all black and I woke up. Not that I wanted to die — but I just wanted all the pain to end." Justin took a deep breath.

Andrew was shocked by what he heard. He never would have realised Nathan's death could have made such an impact on Justin's life.

"As time went on, I kind of got my act together and started working in a fast-food restaurant, where I met Rebecca. She encouraged me to go back to college and I finished my Bachelor's degree and got onto a Master's degree programme. She was the one who found out about this exchange programme studying in Glasgow, which inspired me to apply. Not for a million years did I think I was qualified." Justin's eyes sparkled when he talked about Rebecca.

"I don't dream about the rope and circle any more; recently, I saw the rope in a different way. There were actually two ropes in the circle, which now became two wooden rings. It was like those that a gymnast holds, to swing the bars in order to make a further and higher jump." Justin was relieved when he finally said those last words.

Andrew really felt a sense of this young man's courage and was grateful that he had shared his emotional wounds and dark past with him. He gave Justin a hug to assure him that everything would be all right. "Justin, I'm so sorry to hear that you had such a difficult time after Nathan's death. I'm so glad that you are now on your way to doing great things in your life."

They sat silently for about twenty minutes, their minds now occupied with different memories and thoughts. Then Andrew tried to cheer him up. "Come on, we are going to visit Mama Evelyn. She promised a feast."

"Mr Hughes, could you wait in the car? I just need a few moments alone with Nathan before we leave."

"Of course. Take your time."

Before Andrew walked back to the car, he saw Justin going back to Nathan's grave, where he stood in front of the tombstone with his eyes closed, as if he was communicating with Nathan. While Andrew waited in the car, he thought of what Justin had just shared with him; something he was quite able to relate to.

For a few years after Nathan's death, he was just lost. Many times the pain he felt seemed unbearable. There were many times when he just wanted to scream to rid himself of the pain of knowing he had buried his own son. He felt enormous guilt that his mother lost her own grandson.

Unfortunately, they were not able to share their pain and loss, as they believed they were protecting each other, both afraid that the pain was too much to bear. In their heads, the way they dealt with their pain was by not talking about it as if Nathan didn't even exist. Thinking back, Andrew wished he'd had the courage to talk to his mother about the accident, about their loss and their grief.

"Mr Hughes." Justin knocked on the car window, which brought Andrew back to the present. "Are you okay, Mr Hughes? You look a bit tired." Justin looked worried.

"Oh, thanks. I'm fine. Now we are going to be spoilt with food. I'm going to introduce you to Mrs Evelyn Wang. She was also an important person in Nathan's life. You will like her," Andrew said in a cheerful voice, trying to change the subject as they were leaving the graveyard.

They were both quiet on their way to Mama Evelyn's restaurant. They met Joey as soon as they opened the restaurant door.

"Hi, Andrew! Glad you made it. My mum has been biting my head off because you're not here. I phoned you a few times, but your phone is turned off." Joey seemed visibly relieved that Andrew had finally arrived. He told Andrew his mother had been worried, as he wasn't able to get hold of him.

"Sorry, Joey. My apologies. I was visiting Nathan's grave, so I turned my phone off." Andrew stretched out his arm to shake hands with Joey.

"Oh, let me introduce you." Andrew tilted his head towards Justin. "This is Justin. He was Nathan's best mate in the USA. Come here, Justin. This is Joey, Mrs Wang's eldest son."

Joey looked at Justin and shook his hand. "Nice to meet you."

"Nice to meet you, too."

After that, Joey didn't know what else to say. He led Andrew to a table, where Mama Evelyn was waiting. "Andrew, I have been waiting the whole afternoon." She stood up and grabbed Andrew's hands. "Sit down," she said.

"Mama Evelyn. This is Justin. He was Nathan's neighbour in the USA. He's on an exchange programme in Glasgow. I took him to Nathan's grave today."

Mama Evelyn took a look at Justin and tears started dropping from her face. As she quickly wiped them off, she said, "Okay. No more crying. I'm happy that you're here." She continued, "Sit! I'll ask the chef to prepare some special dishes for you both." Mama Evelyn walked over to the kitchen.

"What a kind-hearted lady. Nathan mentioned Mrs Wang. She was like an extra grandmother to him."

"Yes, she is a special lady. She has always insisted that I, and even Nathan, address her as Mama Evelyn and nothing else." Andrew smiled.

A few minutes later, Joey placed all the dishes that Mama Evelyn had ordered on the table. "Good luck!" He winked and smiled at Andrew and Justin as he put the last dish down.

Mama Evelyn appeared again and encouraged them to start eating. "Eat! Eat!"

At the same time the phone rang, so Mama Evelyn left to answer it. Andrew looked at Justin.

"Come on, Justin, tuck in." Andrew didn't know how, but they managed to finish most of the dishes. He guessed much of the credit went to Justin.

"I have never eaten such good Chinese food."

"You should say that to Mama Evelyn. It will make her happy."

Despite Mama Evelyn and Joey's protests, Andrew and Justin helped to clear the table and then Justin went to the bathroom. Andrew sat down and was checking his phone head down and was surprised when someone took hold of his other hand. Andrew looked up to see Mama Evelyn. "Andrew, tell Mama Evelyn, are you happy?" she asked, seriously and gently.

"Mama Evelyn, we're just friends."

Andrew was taken aback by the question, so he answered it without even thinking. He didn't even know why he said that or why Mama Evelyn had suddenly asked him that question. Luckily, he wasn't sure if Mama Evelyn understood what he had just said. Andrew felt his face turning red and warm.

"Forget your mother, forget Nathan, and forget everything else. Just you, just you, are you happy? It's time for you to find happiness." Mama Evelyn looked into Andrew's eyes with an intensity that made him uneasy.

Andrew tried to figure out how to reply to Mama Evelyn so he didn't have to reveal too much of his true feelings. Her question took him to a deep place. 'Am I happy? Why have I never been in a long-term relationship? What am I afraid of?'

"Mr Hughes, are you all right? You look like you are miles away." Justin returned to the table and Andrew realised Mama Evelyn was no longer there.

'How long have I been on my own?' Andrew thought. 'Mama Evelyn must have left seeing me daydreaming.'

"I am fine. Thanks. Wondering where Mama Evelyn went?" Andrew looked around the restaurant and saw Mama Evelyn approaching their table.

"Did you have enough to eat?" Mama Evelyn returned to the table with a dessert menu in her hand.

"No... can't possibly eat another thing." Both protested at the same time, and all three chuckled.

"Mrs Wang, you look so nice. Your dress — the colour really suits you, and your earrings complement your eyes."

"Oh, you are such a smooth talker. Call me Mama Evelyn." Mama Evelyn was so happy, that she wasn't able to close her mouth from smiling.

'Gosh. Justin is such a charmer,' thought Andrew.

Mama Evelyn then told Andrew about Sami's wedding and hers and Joey's travel arrangements.

"Mama Evelyn, I'll stop by here for lunch next week and I'll book my ticket and accommodation at the same time."

When they were leaving, Mama Evelyn pulled Andrew towards her. "Come over here! Give Mama Evelyn a hug." As he did so, she whispered in his ear, "Enough is enough. It's time for you to find happiness." Andrew almost felt like a child wanting to cry on her shoulder.

After they got home, Andrew was exhausted. "Justin, I'll take a shower first and then I'm off to bed right after." Andrew yawned. After his shower, he went straight to his room. He was reading and ready to sleep when he heard a knock at his door.

"Mr Hughes, may I come in?"

"Of course. Do you need anything to eat or drink?" Andrew was still thinking what to offer Justin. Justin came in and sat carefully on the edge of the bed.

"Mr Hughes, many thanks for taking me to Nathan's grave today."

"You're welcome. I'm happy that you trusted me enough to share the terrible hardships you've had to endure after the accident."

Justin slowly leaned over and gave Andrew a hug; then their lips met. That evening, they spent the night together in the same bed, for the very first time.

The next morning, Andrew woke up a bit earlier than usual, as he didn't quite know how to act in front of Justin after the night before. He got up, took a shower, got dressed and went to the kitchen to make coffee. He was watching the news when he noticed Justin was up.

"Do you want some coffee and brunch?" Andrew shouted to Justin, who was in the bathroom.

'Could one door between us make it less embarrassing?' Andrew tried to convince himself.

"Yes, please, Mr Hughes."

Andrew started making breakfast and was trying out the new smoothie machine he'd bought recently. He chopped up at least five different sorts of fruit and added soya milk. The machine was making such a noise that he hadn't realised that Justin had come into the kitchen and was standing next to him.

"Good morning." Justin tapped on Andrew's shoulder.

"Wow! You scared me a bit."

Andrew poured a glass of smoothie and handed it to Justin. Justin looked at it first. "Okay. Bottoms up!" He drank it all in one go and showed the empty glass to Andrew. "Wow, I've never had something so healthy. You can almost feel the vitamins running through your body when you drink it. Now I need a strong coffee." Justin made a funny face. They both laughed.

"So, what are we going to do today?" Justin asked, trying not to sound awkward.

Andrew cleared his throat. "A few days ago, I was asked to design the interior of a penthouse

157

nearby. I just got the keys to the flat last Friday, so if you want, I can show you it."

"Great, it would be good to see how you work." Justin was excited to see the flat.

"By the way, I forgot to tell you. I've invited Olivia and her husband over for dinner two Saturdays from now. Can you come as well? She said she hasn't seen much of you lately, so I thought it would be a good opportunity for all of us to have a nice dinner together."

"Thanks. I'd like to come. Yes, I've been kind of busy with schoolwork, so I haven't contacted her that much lately. It would be great to catch up."

Justin was so impressed with the penthouse and Andrew's interior design plans. "The owner wants to rip up all the carpets and use the wooden floors that are underneath. He also wants to have a jacuzzi bathtub installed in the en-suite bathroom." Andrew went on to explain all the changes the owner wanted.

"Is there anything I can help out with?" Justin asked.

"I am sure I can think of something. Will I see you next weekend?" Andrew hoped he didn't sound too desperate.

"Oh, I'll have to check. I promised a friend I'd help him move to his new flat."

"Okay. Let me know." Andrew tried not to look or sound too disappointed. At that moment, all Andrew wanted to do was to take Justin in his arms and hug him. He longed for physical closeness, but was afraid of Justin's reaction, as it seemed he didn't want to talk about last night.

They spent a while inside the flat. Then they went for a walk along the Water of Leith and the Dean Village, before heading towards Justin's rental car. It was a small white Hyundai. "Mr Hughes, this is the tyre that got a flat." Justin pointed at the left back wheel.

"Thank God you were okay. I was really worried." Andrew still remembered how terrified he was at the thought that something terrible had happened.

"I wish I hadn't made you worry, but now we have each other's numbers. By the way, thanks for giving me your old smartphone."

"Not at all, you paid for it." Andrew smiled and continued, "Drive carefully now; text me when you get home." Justin walked over and gave Andrew a light hug, before driving off to Glasgow. "Be safe," said Andrew in a voice only he could have heard.

When he got home, he realised how tired he was, as he hadn't slept comfortably the night before. He had kept waking up from time to time, worried that his snoring might disturb Justin. Or, perhaps he just wanted to take a look at Justin lying next to him. 'Was it a dream?'

After he got up from a nap, he collected his thoughts and called Jimi in Spain. "No, you didn't, you dirty old dog," chuckled Jimi, when Andrew told him what had happened. Andrew also heard him telling Vincent, who apparently was sitting next to Jimi, "They did it! They had S.E.X."

"I really don't know what he thinks. He doesn't seem that bothered by it, but also doesn't seem to want to acknowledge it, as we didn't even talk about it this morning," Andrew said to Jimi with uncertainty.

"What are you going to do? Man, remember he's engaged to be married. You have to be careful. I don't want you to get hurt." Jimi sounded worried.

"Don't worry, I won't. Well, I don't know. I just can't stop thinking about him. It's as if he is in my every waking thought," said Andrew, confessing his feelings about Justin for the first time.

"Please, be careful. I don't want you to get hurt. It's also a bit complicated and messy, as he was Nathan's best friend and he knows Olivia, too."

"I know. I'm a bit confused myself, and I need to take some time to think. The good thing is that we won't see each other for another two weeks. He is coming here for dinner with Olivia and her husband on Saturday in a fortnight." Andrew said it as if he was trying to convince himself that he would be okay. "Oh, I bought the ticket to Hong Kong for the wedding.

I got a good deal flying out from Glasgow. I'll come for two weeks."

"Great, see you there. It'll be the first time Vincent has visited Asia, so we will stop first in Bangkok for a week and then go to Hong Kong. After the wedding, we will travel around China for four weeks. All booked and arranged."

Andrew heard Vincent whisper to Jimi, "Ask him who did what to whom last night!"

"You guys are horrible. A gentleman never shares those kinds of details." Andrew chuckled, before saying goodbye, and then hung up. Deep down, Andrew wished he were able to tell the whole world about his night with Justin.

That night, Andrew wasn't able to sleep; partly because he had a nap too late in the afternoon and also because he was thinking about Justin. The scent he had left behind on the bed sheets and pillows didn't help, either.

The next morning, Andrew started contacting all the right tradesmen for the flat, painter, electrician, plumber, carpet and wooden-floor fitter. He worked non-stop, and by Tuesday lunchtime he sent a consolidated quotation to the client for all the work he proposed. The client and Andrew talked over the phone a few times and discussed possible alterations and other options. For the rest of the week he then went to inspect a few of his buy-to-let flats.

By Thursday lunchtime, he got an email from his client accepting his quotation. He then started organising and co-ordinating all the tradesmen and ordering materials. After years of working in this business, he had got to know many reliable tradesmen and worked well with them. Andrew also made an appointment for a plumber to come by to check the drains and pipes in the bathroom and the kitchen.

He sent a message to Justin and shared the good news with him; but although he saw that Justin was online, the reply didn't come until much later that evening. Andrew told himself not to be too sensitive about it, but it was hard.

Justin confirmed that he wouldn't be coming to Edinburgh that weekend. Andrew couldn't help longing for him, as he would not see him for another eight days. He spent the weekend and the next week working in the penthouse. He was at his best when he was busy, but each night before going to bed he thought of Justin and missed him.

Andrew was miserable. It was the first time they hadn't seen each other for that many days since Justin had come in to Andrew's life.

Chapter 12
Step by Step I Am Falling
Part II

The following Friday, Justin arrived around six thirty p.m. Before coming, Justin had already told Andrew that he would rent a car again. "I really enjoy driving." He was trying to convince Andrew of the reasons for renting the car.

"Just be careful, and don't drive too fast." Andrew worried he might have sounded like an old grandad.

Andrew tried to play things down a bit, so as not to show how much he was longing for Justin, and it was actually Justin who gave Andrew a heartfelt hug as soon as he came through the door. Andrew melted and acted normal again.

They had dinner and the conversation flowed as usual, but Andrew could sense Justin was distant. After dinner, they sat and watched TV and ate dessert. Andrew had baked a banana cake and served it with vanilla ice cream, which they both enjoyed. After a while, Justin stood up and said to Andrew, "Mr Hughes, many thanks for the dinner. I've arranged to call

Rebecca via Skype tonight, so I hope you don't mind. I'll be quick and we can watch TV together later."

"Not at all, go ahead." But Andrew was thinking, 'What could I have said? I do mind, and don't call her while you are here.'

Andrew stayed in the living room and could hear voices and laughter coming from Justin's room. He made himself a whisky and tonic. He watched TV for a bit and made himself another one. Andrew then went to the kitchen to do the dishes, came back to the living room and made another drink. Justin still hadn't come out.

Andrew began to feel a bit drunk; so, to clear his head, he went for a shower and then sat in front of the TV again. By then it was about ten-thirty p.m., which meant they had been talking for almost two hours.

'This is ridiculous.' Andrew contemplated whether to wait up or go to bed. He stood up and went to bed. Although his bedroom door was shut, Andrew heard Justin coming out from his bedroom and going into the bathroom. It was a strange feeling in the air, as Andrew didn't know whether he should get up to say good night or at least say something. With all that on his mind, Andrew eventually fell asleep.

The next morning, Justin was up earlier than Andrew; he was woken up by the sound of Justin taking a shower. Andrew got up, got dressed and went to the kitchen to make himself a cup of coffee, which he desperately needed. He still felt a bit drunk after those whisky and tonics he had had the night before.

Justin, with only a towel around his waist, passed by the kitchen on the way back to his room. "Good morning, Mr Hughes," he said.

"Good morning," replied Andrew, his head throbbing.

When Justin came into the kitchen, he apologised for having disappeared the previous night. "I was talking to Rebecca, as she's planning to come visit me here and we were discussing travelling to other parts of Europe."

"Great. I'm sure she'd like Scotland and Europe. Would you like some breakfast?"

"Yes, I'm starving. I could eat a horse." They both smiled, which eased the tension between them.

'How could I ever be angry with him?' thought Andrew.

They were both relaxed and enjoyed breakfast. While helping Andrew with the dishes, Justin said in a very cheerful voice, "Mr Hughes, do you want a massage? I can give you a massage."

It didn't take much to convince Andrew, though he was really confused about what Justin wanted. "Yes, let me first take a shower."

Andrew lay on his stomach and Justin sat on top of him, his hands softly applying pressure to Andrew's head, shoulder, back and arms. Andrew felt and enjoyed every touch and every gentle push from Justin's hand. It was almost as if time had stood still and the world outside this room had no meaning. A while later, Justin asked Andrew to turn over, so now he lay in bed on his back and Justin remained sitting on top of him.

At one point, Andrew took Justin's hand and started slowly kissing it, while Justin was still massaging him with the other. Andrew sat up; they hugged and continued to give each other massages. Inevitably, they took off each other's clothes and no words were needed to express what they wanted to do, at least for Andrew. Andrew was kissing Justin's chest, neck and his ears, and he knew Justin enjoyed it. Andrew went on kissing Justin's lips, when suddenly, and without warning, Justin politely but firmly pushed him away.

"Mr Hughes, I can't do this." Justin stood up, put his clothes on and went back to his room.

'What the fuck!'

He got up and got dressed. At that moment, he craved a cigarette to calm himself down. As he had no cigarettes at home and he hadn't touched them for about forty years, he went to the kitchen instead and made himself a cup a coffee.

He was angry, embarrassed and felt somewhat betrayed.

After about thirty minutes, Justin came out of his room and saw Andrew in the kitchen. "Mr Hughes, I want to make it clear that I'm not gay and I'm engaged to Rebecca, so this can't go on. I like hanging out with you, but I don't think we should give each other massages any more, as I don't want to lead you on and I don't think you should have any feelings for me." Justin was frustrated and it showed in his voice.

"Justin, I haven't forced you to do anything you don't want to. If I have developed feelings for you, it is up to me to deal with it. This is nothing I have predicted or planned and I feel as frustrated as you are. Yes, I do have feelings for you, and there is no one to blame. You can't tell me what I should or should not feel." Andrew spoke in a very angry tone of voice.

Justin was taken aback a bit, as it was the first time he had witnessed Andrew's anger and frustration. "Sorry, Mr Hughes, I just don't want things to get complicated. I'd really like to maintain our friendship." Justin now looked as if he was struggling with his words.

Andrew just didn't know how and to whom he should express his anger. Maybe he was mainly angry with himself, and he knew that he just wanted to hug Justin and never let him go. "Let's not talk about it now. We need to do some grocery shopping.

Olivia and her husband are coming for dinner. Remember?"

They went in Justin's rental car and during the entire journey to the supermarket they were very quiet. Their mood finally lifted a bit once they got there. As they were picking up food items and putting them in the shopping trolley, a thought popped into Andrew's mind. 'When people look at us, what do they think of us? A couple? Friends? Or a father and a son?'

While shopping with Justin, strangely enough, Andrew felt happy and had a sense of belonging; although he knew this sense of belonging or togetherness was not real and could not last.

When Andrew was paying, Justin insisted on buying a cake for dessert and went to pay in a different queue. When they met up again, he handed Andrew a bottle of whisky. "Mr Hughes, just a small token to say thanks for having me stay."

"You didn't need to! That's very considerate of you." Andrew was really touched by the gesture.

When they got back, Justin helped out in the kitchen and set the table. Right after seven p.m., Olivia and her husband, Adrian, arrived. They came by train so they could have a few drinks.

After dinner, they played card games and Olivia caught Justin cheating a few times, which made them all laugh. Olivia and Justin also told Adrian and

Andrew about all the things they had done in the States. They even carefully mentioned Nathan in their stories, and Andrew didn't mind or get upset. The evening was pleasant.

Andrew mentioned to Olivia about the trip to Hong Kong and his itinerary, flying out from Glasgow. "Great. Come a day before so we can spend the evening together and I will drive you to the airport," Olivia said, as she hugged Justin and Andrew goodbye. She looked at Justin. "And you, Justin, you have to report to me every week. You're so busy and I don't see you very often. Don't be a stranger."

"If I were you, I wouldn't argue," Adrian joined in. The four of them laughed.

Once they had gone, Andrew yawned and stretched his hands in the air. "What an evening. I hope you enjoyed it. I'm wiped out. I'll take care of the dishes tomorrow. I'm going to take a shower and go to bed. Is there anything else you need?"

"Mr Hughes, thanks for dinner and a lovely evening. I'm going to watch a bit of TV and then go to bed."

Lying in his room, Andrew reflected on what had happened during the day. He was really puzzled and didn't know how he should feel about Justin. Yes, Justin was engaged to be married, which made his mixed signals even more confusing. 'One minute he wants to be intimate; the next, he pushes me away.

Why are we spending so much time together? Why do we enjoy so much each other's company? What am I doing?' With all these thoughts, Andrew fell asleep.

They both woke up late on Sunday morning, partly due to having a lot to drink the night before. They had brunch at home and headed to the penthouse that Andrew was working on. Justin was very excited about seeing the transformations since his visit a few weeks back. Justin used his rental car to help Andrew throw away lots of junk from the basement and did some small, odd jobs in the property. After a few hours of working, they were both covered in dust and sweat.

"Thanks, Justin, you've done an excellent job. I'd not have been able to do it without you." Seeing Justin so enthusiastic about helping out put Andrew in a good mood. "May I take you out for dinner as a token of my appreciation for your help?"

He approached Justin to give him a hug, as a sign of his gratitude. Justin just held on to that hug. They hugged each other and stroked each other's backs for a very long while. Time stood still. As they held each other, Justin whispered in Andrew's ear, "Mr Hughes, I'm glad I was able to help, as you've been so nice to me, having me to stay and spending time with me."

Andrew slowly pulled away; he didn't want to be tempted to engage in something else that might have spoiled the moment. "Great. Let's go home, get showered and changed."

As Justin was taking a shower, Andrew called and reserved a table at a French restaurant, which was within walking distance. Justin wore a well-fitted turquoise pullover and Andrew wore a shirt, crisply ironed, with silver cufflinks and a dinner jacket. They both looked sharp and were both in a good mood. They enjoyed dinner and the wine recommended by the waiter.

Justin was fascinated and asked many questions about Andrew's experiences in interior design, property management and development. Once again, Andrew thought, 'When people look at us, what do they think? Colleagues, relatives, a couple, friends or a father and a son?' Andrew couldn't help wondering.

Justin told Andrew that the following Monday he would be travelling to London with two classmates from university to visit a company. "We've been invited to meet with people in various levels of management to get some experience in interview skills and get some industrial knowledge for our Master's dissertation."

Andrew was excited and happy for the opportunity for Justin and suggested that he should come down next weekend before travelling to London. Justin agreed. When they got home, they were still in good spirits. Andrew poured two glasses of whisky and tonic and handed one to Justin. Justin took a sip and asked jokingly, "This is a strong one. Are you trying to get me drunk?"

Andrew gave Justin a pretend look of surprise. They both chuckled.

They sat on the sofa in the living room and watched TV. Andrew knew it might upset Justin, but he wasn't able to help himself; he placed his head on Justin's shoulder and held his left hand, gently massaging it with both hands. He noticed that Justin didn't look at him — he just stared at the TV — but Andrew felt he reacted to the massage by holding tightly to his hands.

Moments later, Justin spoke quietly, "Andrew?" Andrew didn't answer, as he didn't know what Justin meant.

With his head hanging down, Justin mumbled, "Andrew, would you mind giving me a massage? My back is a bit sore after today. Or maybe you don't want to? Or maybe we shouldn't?"

Andrew was stunned and surprised, as it was the first time Justin had called him Andrew, and because of what had happened the day before, in addition to the conversation they'd had. His head and heart said, 'No! No! No!' He even heard Jimi screaming 'NO!' at him. But his hands said the opposite. He carefully and gently touched Justin's body. He turned off the TV and slowly led Justin to his bedroom, knowingly taking the risk that Justin might change his mind at any minute or get upset again.

The next morning, Andrew woke up early and got ready. He woke up Justin around eight a.m., as he needed to drive back to Glasgow to return the rental car and then get to his afternoon class. After a quick breakfast, Andrew followed Justin to his car and handed him a bag of food. "Here you are; you can eat this tonight."

"You're too good to me." Justin smiled and patted Andrew on his shoulder.

"Drive carefully, and don't drive too fast. Text me when you get there."

The following week, Andrew was very busy continuing with the renovation work at the penthouse. He hadn't heard anything from Justin, apart from a text on Monday afternoon telling Andrew that he'd arrived safely in Glasgow. Andrew texted back asking what time he'd arrive on Friday, but Justin didn't reply.

He spoke to Jimi about it, but he advised him to wait and let Justin take the initiative. It was hard, especially since that weekend they were supposed to meet up. Up until Friday morning he was still hopeful that Justin might contact him about his arrival. But there was no sign of Justin or any messages from him.

For the first time, Andrew admitted to himself how deeply he had grown to like Justin. They had spent so much time together lately it was bloody hard to go back to his routine of being single. He noticed that Justin was on his mind every waking second. He worked through the weekend in the penthouse, along with the painter and the plumber. He kept himself busy, but couldn't concentrate on much else other than Justin.

He went out with a few friends for dinner on Saturday night. But all he thought about was Justin. Since they'd met, they hadn't been out of contact with each other for this long. As the days went by, Andrew got more and more anxious.

Andrew was in the penthouse on Sunday while waiting for a delivery of a new washing machine and a dishwasher; it hit him how much he missed Justin.

'Something's happened to him? Is he upset with me?' With this unsettling thought in his head, he texted him:

Hi, haven't heard from you in a while. I've been worried. I hope you're not angry with me or something has happened? Hope you are well. Andrew.

Andrew then became busy with the plumber, installing the new appliances, so he didn't check his phone till the late afternoon, and he found a message from Justin.

I have been angry but not at you; rather about what happened. I told you a few times what I don't want, but things still happened. I really care about Rebecca and she means a lot to me and I don't want to hurt her. Maybe it's best we only meet when others are around as well. Justin.

Andrew was furious and had to control his frustration when texting back.

Thanks for being honest. The last thing I want to do is hurt Rebecca. But, have you ever considered my feelings and that I might be hurting, too? I didn't plan things to develop this way and I can't control my feelings for you. I really enjoyed spending time with you and being with you. As well as feeling embarrassed, I feel such a fool. I'm not sure seeing you is a good idea. Maybe we shouldn't see each other for a while. Andrew.

Justin texted right back.

That's a real shame, as I really like seeing you and hanging out with you as a friend. What about we arrange to have dinner together with Olivia and her husband?

Andrew left the penthouse and went for a walk. He felt heavy-hearted and uneasy and needed some fresh air to calm down before replying.

I'm not sure that is a good idea. In order not to make a greater fool of myself, it is best that I don't see you for a while. Take good care of yourself. Andrew.

Another reply from Justin.

It doesn't have to turn out this way. I hope we can still be friends. Justin.

Andrew didn't reply to the last message; he tried very hard to put Justin out of his mind. But the truth was, Andrew missed him, even in his sleep. However, he knew life had to go on. In order to occupy his mind with something else and to keep busy, Andrew took on more projects.

A few days later, Andrew received a few parcels and remembered he had ordered them for Justin as Christmas presents. At first, Andrew didn't know what to do with them and thought it would be awkward to keep them in his house, so he posted them to Justin with a note wishing him well. He had forgotten about it until a few days later, when he received an unexpected text message from Justin:

Thanks for your gifts. I was very surprised when I opened the box. I really like them, the Montblanc fountain pen and rolling pen engraved with my initials. You're too good to me. If you ever need an extra pair of hands for your properties, you know I'd be happy to help. Justin.

Andrew didn't reply; he didn't know what to write. In need of some words of comfort and wisdom, he called Jimi. "Man, this is hard. I really miss him." Andrew sounded really down.

"Andrew, don't beat yourself up about it. I know it's hard, but with time you'll think of him less and less. He's engaged and he's going to get married, so it's best you just let him go on with his journey, whether it's what you want or not."

"The fact is, in a twisted way this pain makes me feel alive. I haven't felt like this for such a long time. If there were a pill I could take to forget about him or the pain, I don't think I'd even take it." Andrew was hoping he didn't sound too pathetic.

"I completely understand, Andrew. Be brave and embrace this experience; although it's hard at the moment, you'll get over it." Jimi continued, "By the way, my mum asked about you. She would like to see you before she and Joey leave for Hong Kong."

With Justin constantly on Andrew's mind, he had totally forgotten about visiting Mama Evelyn.

The last time had been when he had brought Justin there with him. "I'll stop by the restaurant tomorrow, and I can't wait to see you in Hong Kong."

"Yes, we're going to have fun. I'm sure I can introduce you to some young Asians that are looking for an older Western sugar daddy." Jimi laughed so much he almost dropped his phone.

"You're such a wanker." Andrew laughed, too. Before they said their goodbyes, he asked Jimi, "Do you remember when we came out to our mothers about twelve years ago?" Andrew was pleased he finally came out to his mother before she passed away, as much as he regretted, he didn't share it with Nathan in time.

After they hung up, Andrew's mind was then drawn to the event that took place twelve years ago. 'I must have looked good in the closet. Nobody had a clue. The only regret I had was that I didn't have the chance to share that part of my life with Nathan.'

The way Jimi and Andrew had stepped out of the closet, and the event and circumstances that led to their unintentionally coming out twelve years ago in their late thirties had been a humorous turn of events. Andrew had got there with Jimi's help, and he had planned to tell his son face to face as well, but never got the chance, as Nathan died a few months after Andrew and Jimi came out to their mothers.

Chapter 13
What Does Not Kill Us Only Makes Us Stronger

As soon as Andrew entered the restaurant, Mama Evelyn pulled him to her and gave him a massive hug. His mother was standing next to her, smiling. Andrew approached her and gave his mother a hug and realised she had a new perm and had even put make-up on. He stepped back a bit and took a good look at both of them and complimented them on their new hair and their dresses.

"Aren't you both looking beautiful tonight! What's the occasion?"

Hilary blushed and seemed visibly less comfortable than Evelyn. Evelyn, as usual, was in full make-up, wearing her trademark bright red lipstick. Although Evelyn and Hilary were of a similar age, Evelyn had always dressed in more daring colourful outfits and accessories.

Andrew looked around for clues. 'Have I forgotten someone's birthday?' Then he said jokingly to Mama Evelyn, "Wow! I'm blinded by the jewels you're wearing!" Hilary and Evelyn looked at each other and then giggled like two schoolgirls.

Andrew remembered the text he had received from Jimi earlier and he passed on the message. "Mama Evelyn, Jimi won't make it tonight. His flight from Geneva has been cancelled due to a pilot strike." Andrew continued, "But his ticket has been rebooked and they put him on another flight and he'll be here tomorrow."

Evelyn replied, feigning anger, "Yes, he called me and I already yelled at him for missing tonight's dinner."

Evelyn and Hilary were still holding one of Andrew's arms and led him to a huge table, set for eight people. "Who else is coming?" asked Andrew.

"Some friends," answered Evelyn, as she looked at Hilary; both giggled again and were not able to hide their excitement.

Andrew looked at his mother for an explanation, but she just patted his shoulder and pulled him down into a chair. The two women then carried on with their preparations, making sure the table was perfectly set; running back and forth, putting wine bottles and other soft drinks on the table.

As Andrew was not allowed to help, he texted Jimi:

I am at the restaurant now and our mums are acting very strangely. Do you know anything special about tonight's dinner? Andrew.

Jimi replied: *?*

About twenty minutes later, the entrance door of the restaurant opened and six people came in, two young ladies and four older adults. Mama Evelyn ran to the entrance to greet the guests and Andrew noticed his mother nervously straightening up the collar of her dress. 'Really. What is the big deal?' he wondered.

Mama Evelyn's excitement made him think that they must be quite important guests. He stood up as they approached the table. As he turned his head, Andrew saw his mother also warmly greeting the newcomers.

'Oh, they must be the friends Mama Evelyn mentioned.' In his head, Andrew was still puzzled as to what was going on. 'Does my mother know these people as well? Strange, she never mentioned it.'

He felt a gentle nudge on his back from his mother and realised he had to stop daydreaming. He went up to them and shook hands with everyone, as he didn't want to embarrass Mama Evelyn or his mother. They all nodded to each other as a greeting gesture, so Andrew reciprocated.

Once they sat down, Mama Evelyn introduced herself, Andrew and Hilary to the guests, especially to the four older adults, and asked Andrew to pour the wine for everyone. For some reason he felt uncomfortable and sensed that all eyes were on him. 'Where is that damn Jimi?'

As soon as the conversation started, Andrew found out that they were from Singapore and that the two young ladies were cousins, who were studying here in Edinburgh. Their parents were visiting them. The two young ladies had been to the restaurant a few times before and got to know Mama Evelyn and Hilary. Andrew listened to their conversations but didn't say a word, because he still didn't have a clue as to what was going on or why he was invited to this dinner. He had no idea who they were, and his mother had never mentioned them before.

The two young ladies talked about their studies and joked about how they were enjoying living in Edinburgh, away from their parents. Everyone laughed politely and nodded again to each other, so Andrew did as well. From their initial appearance, based on how they were dressed and their good manners, Andrew had the impression that they were both from wealthy and respectable families.

So far, Hilary was sitting there smiling, quiet but looking excited. Mama Evelyn made apologies for her son not being there, but promised to organise another dinner. Mama Evelyn was doing most of the talking. It was almost like a one-woman show. Dishes started to be served, lobster with crispy noodles Hong Kong-style (Andrew's favourite), steamed fish with ginger and spring onion, imperial ribs, crispy duck and many other dishes. Andrew lost count. Mama Evelyn encouraged the guests to start, and asked Andrew to pour the wine for everyone. After lots of "Please, you first" and "No, after you", everyone started eating.

For the first time, Andrew took a close look at the young ladies. They were beautiful and possessed that confidence and energy which young and privileged people in their early to mid-twenties seemed to have. During the meal, all six parents were talking; the two young ladies were talking and laughing quietly among themselves about something. Andrew was busy listening and enjoying the feast. Finally, Andrew's name came up, and it was Mama Evelyn who introduced him to the guests again.

"Andrew is a very successful property developer and an interior designer here in Edinburgh. He owns his own company. He is not married and has a son who is studying in the USA."

Evelyn exaggerated Andrew's good qualities, but Hilary tried to tone it down a bit. It felt to Andrew like a sales team trying to sell off and get rid of damaged or second-rate goods.

Andrew had a sense of panic. He felt sick. The realisation finally dawned on him that he'd been set up on a blind date. He looked up and met the two young ladies' eyes; from their looks, he realised they, too, had noticed, having had no idea about the real purpose of the dinner, either.

'Oh, Good Lord, what are they doing to me? I wish Jimi was here.' Andrew's mind was filled with questions. He sat there feeling uncomfortable for the rest of the evening and only answered questions when he was spoken to, avoiding eye contact with any of them when replying. When the dinner was finally over, Andrew was beyond exhausted.

As the guests went to leave, they all followed them out, saying their goodbyes so many times Andrew lost count. Once they had left, Mama Evelyn dragged Andrew by his arm, led him back to the table and sat him down. "What do you think about the two young ladies?" she asked.

Hilary didn't say a word. She sat next to Andrew and waited intently for an answer from him, which made him even more uncomfortable. "What do you mean?" Andrew was almost in tears.

"Don't you think they're beautiful?" asked Mama Evelyn. "You know," she continued, "first, I thought the taller one for you and the other for Jimi, but as Jimi's not here it is his own fault, so you can choose first."

"Choose what?" Now Andrew really wanted to cry and was really frustrated with Jimi for not being there.

"Don't be shy," said Hilary gently, looking at Andrew.

"Mum, don't be silly. I don't know these people," Andrew protested.

"Don't worry; they'll be here for another month. If you'd like, you can start to get to know them before they return to Singapore. Maybe you will like one of them, and who knows?" said Mama Evelyn in a convincing voice.

Now, Andrew felt he had to make it clear. "Now, stop it! It's ridiculous. I can't believe you two set me up on a blind date!"

Hilary put her hand over Andrew's. "Andrew, we just thought it would be a great opportunity for you to get to know them and perhaps find a special woman in your life and even get married." Hilary looked at Evelyn for support.

"Yes, we just want you to be happy. We've already spoken to Nathan about it, and he agreed."

"Please, don't involve me in this. I can't believe you already spoke to Nathan about it. When I'm ready and the right person comes along, I'll let you know." Andrew was almost shouting as his frustration grew.

"Okay, okay. We're just trying to help." They said it with such innocence, it made Andrew feel a little guilty, as he knew they had the best intentions.

"Thank you both for doing this, but this is not for me," he said.

"Maybe Jimi would like to be introduced to them?" asked Mama Evelyn in a hopeful voice.

As Andrew looked back at them, he could tell his mother was disappointed, but Mama Evelyn still seemed to have some ideas up her sleeve.

'I hope Jimi won't be upset about the blind date set-up. I'd better warn him before he returns home tomorrow.'

When Andrew got home, he called Jimi and told him about the evening; Jimi just laughed and laughed. They remembered how Mama Evelyn had even arranged a few unsuccessful blind dates for Hilary in the past.

"Can you believe it? Once when I was younger my mum handed me a photo of a young Asian girl I'd never met before, asking me what I thought of her. I didn't say anything special and didn't pay much attention to it, throwing the photo in the bin. After a few weeks, my mum asked me whether I wanted to meet the girl, but I'd totally forgotten about it. My mum wasn't amused, so she asked for the photo back. She was furious when I told her that I'd thrown it away. My mum then started preaching to me that in

Asian culture only a husband could have photos of his wife."

Although Andrew couldn't see it, he was sure Jimi was rolling his eyes as he was telling the story. "If one day I was to show that picture to a husband of hers, it will be seen as a disgrace to his wife that another man was in possession of her photo." Jimi sighed.

Later, Jimi learned from others that his mum had had to make up stories to the girl's parents about how the photo had got lost and she had had to apologise profusely.

"I can't believe she is doing this again after what happened the last time. Sami told me that she tried to set her up as well, and she refused to be part of it." Jimi showed the frustration in his voice. At that moment, Andrew felt a strong need to see Jimi as soon as he landed the next day. "Jimi, I'll meet you at the airport tomorrow, 'cause I've something to tell you."

"Great! See you tomorrow. I've something I need to tell you, too."

Before they hung up, Jimi asked Andrew to double-check the flight schedule before coming to the airport, to be sure it had not been cancelled again. "If your flight is cancelled again and you don't come home tomorrow, I think your mother will disown you," Andrew warned Jimi, and they both laughed.

At this point in time, Andrew felt he needed to come out to Jimi. He was worried that it might be a difficult conversation, but as they had been friends for so long, he was hoping it wouldn't be an issue. All the same, in his head he was turning over what Jimi might say about his sexuality; more from curiosity than worry.

Andrew had known that he was gay from a very early age, but until now he didn't come out to his mother or anyone else that knew him. He did go out on the gay scene, but never really felt he fitted in; he was a lousy drinker and didn't smoke. When Andrew started to go out in those circles, it was kind of expected to hide one's shyness or insecurities with alcohol and cigarettes. He tried smoking a few times, but didn't want to come home smelling of cigarettes, especially around Nathan, so he quit. He didn't like the financial aspect of it, either. In the beginning, when Andrew was raising Nathan, he didn't always have a steady job, so for him to waste money he didn't have on alcohol and cigarettes was irresponsible and unthinkable.

He made some gay friends and formed a few short-term relationships with some men, but didn't feel he could bring any of them home to meet his mother; plus, he was in the closet at that time. Over the years, he lost contact with most of them. Not that it was anyone's fault; people change and grow apart.

One might say Andrew had always been a loner. As he grew older, he felt much more comfortable about not being the norm. He didn't have to pretend to be someone else or bend and compromise his values to fit in.

When Andrew was in his mid-twenties, he became a volunteer for a gay helpline, a resource for those, especially the young, trying to fit in and be accepted, and for those who were dealing with drug addiction, alcoholism and depression. From those conversations and also his own observations, he discovered there was pressure within the gay community; many gay men seemed to be unsure of themselves and felt insecure. Unfortunately, one of the ways to manage their insecurities was to put others down or to gossip about them.

He discussed this issue with a few friends, saying maybe it was just human nature and that we all judge others one way or another and want sympathy when we are the "victim" of harsh judgements. But it still puzzled Andrew why as a community, some gay people didn't care to be more tolerant and accepting of one another.

In the mid-1990s, Andrew, for the first time, had a place of his own. While Sami looked after Nathan, he took on voluntary work preparing meals once a week for people living with HIV and their family members and friends. The centre was created as a refuge where people could come and stay for a few days to get away and escape their daily lives. Andrew really enjoyed working there, and it was an opportunity for him to use his cookery skills, especially with influences of Asian/Scottish cuisine. He also liked the challenge of preparing food for as many as thirty guests and staff members. After Andrew had been volunteering a few times, a guest at first hesitantly and shyly approached him and thanked him for the meals he prepared.

"Oh, you are most welcome. I'm happy you like them. Here, try my bread pudding. This is the first time I've made it. Hope it's not too sweet." Andrew handed the guest a plate after they sat down in the living room. Andrew had sensed the guest's need to talk.

"Andrew, I've tried your food a few times now and I really like how you use seasoning and present your dishes." The guest stopped and just stared at the bread pudding Andrew had handed him.

"Take your time." Andrew could see that the guest was visibly emotional and down, but despite that there was still a sparkle and some mischief in his eyes, which came through when he spoke about Andrew's cooking.

"I've been depressed and stressed out ever since I found out I was HIV positive. I haven't told or talked to many people; I'm scared of how they will react. I don't have any appetite because of the combination of medications I am taking, but now I have something to look forward to when I visit the centre."

There it was. Andrew saw a smile. "I'm so pleased that my food made you feel better. Tell me what other dishes you would like me to make next time." Andrew was really touched to learn that his cooking had a positive impact on people.

As Andrew was leaving, the duty manager approached him. "Andrew, I'm so pleased with your progress and that you've made a connection with that guest. He's been coming here regularly for the past month, but he hasn't been keen to open up or talk to any of us or any of the other guests."

As the duty manager was talking, Andrew was already thinking about recipes for the next Sunday's meals. "Great. I've promised to cook a beef stroganoff the next time I come here; the same way he told me his mother used to make it when she was alive. He told me he was very close to her."

The next time he arrived, Andrew was immediately told by the staff at the centre that the guest he had been talking to had taken his own life. He had hanged himself a few days earlier in a flat that he had recently moved into. He hadn't even unpacked any of the boxes. Andrew was heartbroken when he received the news. After that day, he became tearful whenever he thought about him and their brief chats together.

He found out that a few months ago the guy had been kicked out by his partner, whom he had been living with for many years, and none of his family wanted to know anything about him when they found out he was HIV positive.

While volunteering for the centre, Andrew heard many cruel and sad stories from the visiting guests. It was a mad era during that time, as so many people were unknowingly infected with HIV and so many of them died from it when it developed into AIDS. They experienced fear and shame and were often mistreated by society, work places and at times even their loved ones.

From time to time, Andrew still thought about the guest and all the other guests who he had cooked for and their stories, and wondered how their lives and fates unfolded.

"You don't only cook with your hands. You cook with your heart." Those were the last words that had been said to Andrew by the guest now many years ago, and they were words Andrew would cherish for the rest of his life.

Still unresolved about coming out to Jimi, the next day Andrew set out to meet him at the airport. Andrew didn't have to wait too long, as the flight landed about twenty minutes ahead of schedule.

As soon as Jimi saw Andrew, he walked quickly towards him and gave him a hug. "Hello, Andy boy." Jimi called out a nickname he had had for Andrew since they were small. He held Andrew tight briefly and tried to mess up Andrew's hair with his hand. Andrew managed to turn away his head and then peeled away from Jimi's hug.

"I'm glad I got here early." He took a closer look at Jimi, who was crisply and sharply dressed, as usual, with not one piece of hair misplaced on his head. "You don't look like you have just been travelling!" Andrew said it to tease Jimi, but he was impressed.

"For some reason I got upgraded to business class in the front row and didn't have any checked-in luggage, so I was able to get out as quickly as I could." Jimi said it with a smile, a smile that he had had since childhood and which gave Andrew a bit more confidence for what he was about to say.

Andrew headed to a café in the arrival hall and Jimi followed, a sign that he wanted to speak to Jimi before leaving the airport. Andrew ordered two cups of coffee and pointed at a free table for them to sit down.

"What is it? Can't we talk on the way home or at your place?" Jimi took a large sip of the coffee, puzzled by the urgency.

Though Andrew had butterflies in his stomach, he felt he needed to share this coming out with his lifelong best friend.

"Well, Jimi Wang, I've known you for most of my life and you're like a brother to me, so I am about to share something about myself with you." Andrew spoke anxiously, avoiding Jimi's eyes. Jimi didn't say anything, but Andrew could feel him staring at him in anticipation, waiting for him to continue, which made the situation even more tense for Andrew.

"I… okay, I'm just going to say it... I am… I… I am gay and I haven't come out." Despite being nervous, Andrew found the courage to force out the words in the end.

Jimi didn't seem particularly surprised. "Do you want to hear something funny?" Andrew looked up at Jimi. "Actually, I'm gay, too." Jimi said it with such ease. Andrew was the one who now looked shocked. It took him a while to digest and evaluate this and whether or not Jimi was pulling his leg.

Jimi had always been popular with girls ever since Andrew had known him. Like his father, Jimi grew up to be a tall and beautiful man, with dark thick hair and deep features. Jimi was Mr Popular in school and was always invited to parties; Andrew was just a tag-along. Andrew had seen Jimi many times going to a room with girls at parties, even in their early teens.

What Jimi didn't know was that Andrew had even fancied Jimi when they were very young. Once, when they were playing hide and seek, Jimi found Andrew and somehow gave him a quick kiss on the lips. Without thinking, Andrew wanted to kiss him back, but Jimi just pushed Andrew away and told him not to be silly.

"I always knew deep down that I was gay. Did you ever suspect I was gay?" Andrew asked, curious.

"I found out that I was gay when I went to college. Actually, I considered it briefly about you, but as I was not out, I didn't want to open that Pandora's box of thoughts." Then Jimi added, "I figured out you were gay a long time ago; you walk funny," intending to tease. They both chuckled out of a sense of relief. Somehow the tension just melted.

"You're such a wanker," Andrew said. "Do you remember Greg from school?"

"Greg... oh, yes, the bully." It took a while for Jimi to remember who Greg was. "I thought he and his family moved to England when we were about thirteen or fourteen."

Greg Stevens was the tallest and biggest in their class. He was always a troublemaker in school. He picked on girls and pupils who were smaller than he was. He was a headache for many teachers as well;

he always made inappropriate remarks and asked annoying questions during lessons, just to get attention and a reaction.

"Yes, he moved back to Scotland. I met him a few weeks ago," said Andrew. "He contacted me out of the blue, asking me to help him and his family to find a larger home. He must have found me through my business website. He's been married and divorced twice and has one son each with his respective ex-wives. His current girlfriend, who's twenty years his junior, has just given birth to their second child, just a few weeks before he got in touch with me."

Jimi listened, but Andrew could see Jimi wasn't that interested in this story. Jimi didn't like Greg for a reason. He'd heard on several occasions that he had called them both faggots behind their backs as they walked by, just because Andrew and Jimi had always hung out together.

"Guess what, we had dinner together one evening a few weeks ago and then he wanted to come over to my place afterwards."

Jimi almost dropped his coffee and, seeing the astonishment in his eyes, Andrew continued, "We met first in a bar. He was actually very polite and pleasant. He apologised for his past behaviour in school. He told me that he'd had a very abusive upbringing. His mother ran away with some other guy. As he was the youngest, his father and two older brothers bullied him. He also asked about you. I told him that you are now a 'big shot' working for the United Nations and living in Geneva, Switzerland."

"Poor guy." Jimi sounded only somewhat sympathetic, which was understandable. Greg was someone really difficult to like. Then Jimi urged Andrew, "And?"

"Well, we had a nice meal later that evening and he told me about his two failed marriages and that his current girlfriend had just given birth to their second child. He now has four kids, all boys. He told me he was beyond exhausted and was happy to get out of the house for a bit; away from screaming babies and his girlfriend's shouting and constant arguing."

Andrew finished his coffee and went on with the story. "That poor guy. He said he hadn't had a good night's sleep for years and he was on anti-depressants!"

Andrew could tell that Jimi didn't seem that concerned, but he continued, "He knew that I'd had Nathan when I was nineteen. We had such a heart-to-heart conversation. Surprisingly, when he asked me about my life, maybe it was the alcohol, I actually felt quite comfortable telling him I was gay." Andrew lowered his voice.

"What! I can't believe you came out to him before you came out to me!" Jimi joked.

"To my surprise, he didn't seem to have any problem with it. We had a really good chat. I think in the end he'd had a bit too much to drink. We were walking down a dark alley towards his bus stop and I was about to give him a friendly goodbye hug, when he suddenly grabbed me and tried to kiss me. He then asked whether he could come back to my place."

"What did you say?" Now Jimi was really interested.

"I told him that my standards are pretty low, but I have standards." Andrew laughed. "No, I'm only kidding. I said maybe it wasn't such a good idea, as his girlfriend would be at home waiting for him and, for God sake, she has just given birth."

Andrew blushed a bit and said, "Don't get me wrong; he is a good-looking guy and I was tempted, but I didn't want to get involved in that messy life of his. I called him a few days later just to ask how he was doing and to update him about a new house I had found for him. I tried his number a few times, but wasn't able to get through, and then realised he had blocked my number." Andrew raised his voice. "Can you believe it? He blocked my number!"

They laughed so hard they had to gasp for air.

Andrew said in a sad and serious voice, "You know what he told me? He said he constantly argued with his girlfriend and was never able to satisfy her. If he did nine out of ten things right, she complained about the one thing he had done wrong. If he did all ten things right, she complained about his previous mistakes. If he did everything correctly in accordance with her demands, she then told him she had dreamt he had done something wrong." Andrew started laughing and wasn't able to stop for a while.

"What?"

Andrew dried off his tears. "It reminds me of a joke I heard. A wife bought two ties and gave them to her husband for his birthday. The next day he wore one of the ties. She looked at him and then disapprovingly said to him, 'So you don't like the other one?'"

Jimi shook his head in disbelief.

"Oh, my goodness, that poor guy. Now he's forced to live in the closet with a girlfriend, two ex-wives and four children." Jimi continued in a serious tone of voice, "Not in a million years did I think Greg was gay or bi-sexual. You just don't know, do you? Either way, he'll struggle all his life wondering whether or not to come out. I really hope he has the courage to, but then he has his children to consider. I don't know about you, but I'm so thankful that I haven't gone down that path, getting married and having children."

"Me, too. I can't imagine that, especially since I don't want to hurt any innocent woman just to make myself be normal in everyone's eyes." Andrew couldn't agree more.

They then exchanged stories about sexual experiences and boyfriends. Some of Jimi's stories made Andrew blush. He realised Jimi was much more experienced and adventurous; he was so much more comfortable in his own skin than Andrew.

"Do you remember Vincent, who you met at my party?" Jimi asked curiously.

Andrew nodded his head.

"Vincent is my boyfriend and we've been together for almost three years. We're seriously considering having a child through surrogacy." Jimi's face lit up.

"Good for you," Andrew said.

"And, what about you? Do you have someone in your life?"

"No, not at the moment; no one wants me!" Andrew made a sad face.

"You're such a passive aggressive tosser. By the way, do you want me to set you up with someone?"

"NO! Stop it, and I mean it. For heaven's sake, you are worse than your mother," Andrew warned Jimi seriously.

"Okay. You will find someone when the time's right. He would be the luckiest person in the world. Though he would have to put up with your snoring." Jimi chuckled.

"I don't snore. By the way, what should we tell our mothers?" Andrew asked.

"Well, why don't we tell them together?" Jimi sounded very excited.

"Are you sure they can take it?" Andrew was worried.

"They'll be fine, and if we tell them together, at least they don't have to get shocked twice." Jimi smiled and continued, "But please don't say anything about Vincent yet. I want to take it one step at a time." Jimi gave Andrew a long, warm and encouraging hug.

They went back to Andrew's flat to drop off Jimi's hand luggage first, as he would be staying with Andrew while he visited Edinburgh.

Although Jimi said that it would be no problem coming out and telling his mother he was gay, he took a few shots of vodka.

"Here, you will need this." Jimi handed Andrew a shot.

"Actually, what I didn't tell you was Vincent's coming-out-to-his-parents experience. Although his parents have gay friends, they didn't take it very well when Vincent finally told them he was gay after our relationship became stable. They took the coming-out event quite well, or so it seemed. They told him they loved him no matter what; but after that, they had a somewhat cold relationship. They never asked about his life and never acknowledged my existence, although Vincent told them about me and that we were together."

Jimi's voice saddened. "His siblings are a bit better, but there is a thin layer of distance that he visibly noticed once he told them. It's so not fair on Vincent." Jimi became quiet.

"Now you are telling me. Maybe we should wait a bit longer?" Andrew sounded troubled and hesitant. He drained the vodka shot and then shook his head, making a disgusted facial expression.

"What! You want to go on another blind date organised by my mum? Don't worry, we are doing it together and we have each other." Jimi raised his voice and poured himself another shot.

"I really hope they will take the news well, with no dramatic scenes or tears. I hope we are doing the right thing. What if they disown us?" Andrew mumbled.

"Well, what doesn't kill them will only make them stronger. It is now or never."

With his eyes open as big as a soldier about to go into battle, Jimi swallowed another shot of vodka and slammed the shot glass firmly on the table.

They went to the restaurant in the early afternoon because they wanted to arrive before it started to get busy. Mama Evelyn gave Andrew a hug as she saw them enter, but she didn't even look at her own son. She then turned and walked towards the back of the restaurant.

"Oh, Jimi, so nice to see you," said Hilary. "We know you didn't mean to miss the dinner last night and it wasn't your fault. But your mother was worried." Hilary gave Andrew and Jimi a hug and led them to a table in the back. The two of them carefully sat down at the table where Evelyn sat. Hilary looked at all three of them, smiled and then sat next to Andrew.

"You really missed an important event last night," said Mama Evelyn, pretending to be angry. She put her hand on Jimi's shoulders and looked at Andrew. "Are you thirsty?"

Without waiting for an answer, she went to the bar and made Chinese herbal tea and poured them all a cup. "Now, there's still a chance for you to meet the young ladies and their parents. How long are you staying for, so I can plan?" Mama Evelyn wanted to know.

"Mum and Mrs Hughes, there is something Andrew and I need to tell you."

Both women said "What?" at the same time.

There was silence for a few moments, until they both repeated "What?"

"Well…" Jimi hesitated. "Andrew and I want to tell you that…"

"What is it?" interrupted Mama Evelyn.

Silence…

Now Hilary looked at Andrew and seemed worried.

"Okay, here it comes... Andrew and I... Andrew and I are gay and we want you to know, because we love you."

Andrew looked down at the table, avoiding eye contact with everyone. 'I am so proud of Jimi,' he thought. 'And so relieved that I didn't have to announce it myself.'

There was silence again.

Andrew looked around and saw that both Mama Evelyn and his mum seemed to be okay and had taken the announcement well; but he could also see that there were hundreds of thoughts running through Mama Evelyn's mind.

"So, you're both gay?" she asked.

"Yes," said Andrew, feeling like it was his turn to speak. "We really wanted to share it with you both because we love you and we don't want to hide it from you any more," adding quickly, "and I will tell Nathan myself when he's back next time."

Without hesitation, Hilary leaned over and gave Andrew a heartfelt hug. "I love you, son," she said tenderly in his ear.

It was a rare occasion for Hilary to show her affection towards her son in public, which made him a bit teary and emotional and shy, as he had just come out to his mother. At the same time, Andrew felt as if a ton of weight had been lifted from his shoulders and he was able, for the first time in his life, to be honest with her about who he truly was.

"Wait, so you're both gay and you're a couple?" asked Mama Evelyn in a very excited and hopeful tone.

A little stunned, neither Jimi nor Andrew expected that question and couldn't understand why she would think that. "No, Mama Evelyn. We are both gay, but we're not a couple," Andrew said.

"Why? Don't you like my son? What is wrong with Jimi? I thought you both get along well?" She sounded a little confused and disappointed.

"No, Mama Evelyn. We like each other like brothers." Andrew looked at Jimi for support and kicked him under the table.

Jimi took a turn in trying to explain to his mother. "Mum, we're good friends, but we only just came out to each other this morning after I arrived."

"So, you might be a couple in the future?"

'For heaven's sake. This woman doesn't give up,' thought Andrew. Without even thinking, and in a subconscious attempt to divert attention from himself, he blurted out, "No, Mama Evelyn... we don't like each other in that way. Besides, Jimi has a boyfriend called Vincent, and they are seriously considering having a child together through surrogacy."

There was a short silence. Andrew saw the look on Jimi's face and realised that he wanted to strangle him.

Hilary stood up, went over to Jimi and gave him a huge hug. She then put her arms around the two boys.

"Okay, now I know. As a mother, I'm always the last to know. Now at least I know my place." Mama Evelyn didn't look at Jimi, but turned her head away as her way of showing she was upset.

As Joey was the first-born, he was a joy to his grandmother, old Mrs Wang, and they were very close. She had cared for him and looked after him from birth, as Evelyn had gone back to work right after she was physically able. She couldn't afford to stay home too long after the birth. Family Wang needed money.

Sami, on the other hand, was very much Edmond's little girl. It was extremely hard for her when their parents got divorced. She kept in close touch with her father and visited him almost daily when he was living in the care home before he died.

So, Jimi was actually the closest of the three children to Mama Evelyn. Jimi was the youngest in the family for ten years before Sami was born, so he and Mama Evelyn developed a close bond. Jimi remained a mummy's boy even though he was almost in his forties, so it was understandable that Mama

Evelyn felt left out and excluded from his life, especially as Jimi had moved away to London to go to university and then moved to Geneva for work.

"Mummy, don't be like that. I was going to tell you, but I wanted to wait for the right moment," pleaded Jimi.

He always found it difficult to handle his mother's dramatic outbursts. He held her hands and said with sincerity, "I'm sorry I haven't been honest with you, but I didn't want to worry or upset you. I don't say it often enough, but I love you, Mummy."

Tears were running down Jimi's face, and Andrew looked over at Mama Evelyn to see that she was crying quietly, too. They all sat in silence, not knowing what to say, till Mama Evelyn asked Jimi gently, "What is Vincent like? When can I meet him?"

"Mum, Vincent is French, originally from Paris. He works for the Red Cross and lives in Lausanne, a city next to Geneva."

Everyone could see the sparkle in Jimi's eyes when he talked about Vincent. Jimi took out his wallet and pulled out two photos of him and Vincent on holiday in France earlier that year. Jimi told the story of how and where they met and what plans they had for the future.

At this point, everyone was looking at the photos and asking about Vincent. It had become Jimi's show, but Andrew was happy that he wasn't the one at the centre of attention. Mama Evelyn looked intently into Jimi's eyes. "Next time you come home, you bring Vincent with you." It was more of an order than an invitation.

At that point, in order to end the coming-out episode, Jimi announced, "Blimey, I'm so hungry!"

Mama Evelyn and Hilary quickly stood up, rushed into the kitchen and ordered food for their sons. As Jimi and Andrew were shovelling food into their mouths, Mama Evelyn talked softly to Jimi, while Hilary carefully and shyly asked Andrew more about his life.

Though feeling relief that he had finally come out to his mother, Andrew wished he had more cheerful news to share. Suddenly, he felt a little ashamed and sad that he didn't have anyone in his life. Andrew had had a few brief relationships, but for one reason or another he always ended it before it developed into something more serious.

As Jimi and Mama Evelyn were still talking, Andrew and Hilary just sat there, staring at the table; their minds were in totally different places. 'Why do I push people away? Am I afraid of rejection? Is it easier for me to end it first? Has it been my own doing that I am alone?' Thoughts were filling Andrew's head.

Hilary tried to break the silence. "How is Nathan? Have you heard from him?"

"Nathan is fine," Andrew replied abruptly. "He told me that he wants to apply for a full scholarship and transfer from a community college to a state college." Hearing this, Jimi and Mama Evelyn turned to them and began asking about Nathan, too.

Mama Evelyn and Hilary soon found they were needed back in the kitchen and at the front of house. Andrew and Jimi finally had a chance to relax and talk to each other. Later that evening, they drank lots of wine and were both in good spirits.

"Nathan and I really loved our trip to Geneva," said Andrew. "I hope things got sorted out with the insurance company?"

"Yes, thank God. After lots of delays and protest letters from a friend of mine who is a lawyer, also working for the UN, I finally received reimbursement for the claim. The case was extra complicated because there hadn't been a break-in; but your statement helped. The bastards! As if it wasn't enough to steal my underwear collection, they even took the ones that were in the wash."

Andrew wanted to laugh about the worn underwear, but managed to behave himself.

Jimi also told Andrew that he had had nightmares for a while afterwards and found himself constantly checking the locks on his door in the middle of the night, even though they had been changed. He had even gone to a few counselling sessions for post-traumatic stress.

Andrew lightened the mood, saying, "The thief must have had very low standards or a strange fetish to steal your smelly, worn underwear." They laughed hysterically at that.

Andrew looked at Jimi with such admiration. He knew he wouldn't have been able to come out if it hadn't been for Jimi. He felt that the day could not have gone better... until Mama Evelyn reappeared. "What am I going to tell those two young ladies and their parents? Oh, and I forgot to tell you both that I've invited them over for dinner again tomorrow."

Chapter 14
A Broken Heart

In the weeks that followed the painful and conclusive of texts Andrew had with Justin, he drowned himself in work; he needed to escape from his feeling of frustration, and his broken heart.

Andrew worked very hard on the project for professional reasons; to keep up his good reputation, but also because he felt he had to channel his thoughts and energy. He just wanted to come home tired after a day's work and then go straight to bed. He hadn't felt this lonely in years.

There were times when he almost texted Justin, but refrained from doing so at the last moment, mostly because he didn't want to make an even bigger fool of himself, but also because he was hoping for a miracle where Justin would take the initiative and contact him.

The renovation works for the penthouse were almost complete and the owners were happy with the progress and results.

One evening, he visited Mama Evelyn and Joey before they left for Hong Kong. "Mama Evelyn, do you mind having this? I went through the boxes of my mother's belongings the other day and found it." Andrew handed her an elegant jewellery box.

Mama Evelyn vaguely remembered that she had seen this jewellery box before, as Hilary had shown it to her once. She carefully opened it and saw a pearl necklace. "I can't accept this," she said, and put the box back into Andrew's hands. She had recognised it and thought it might be the last piece of Hilary's jewellery that Andrew had.

Andrew hadn't been able to sort through or throw away all of Hilary's belongings right after her passing. Without even noticing it, as part of the grieving process he only sorted them and threw or gave away items from time and time.

Right after Hilary's death, Andrew found some gold chains and jewellery items while clearing her home. He didn't know what to do with them, so he had asked Mama Evelyn what she thought.

"Don't you want to keep them?" Mama Evelyn had asked, as she was worried Andrew might regret one day not having kept them.

"It is not like I have someone to pass them on to." Andrew shook his head. He decided to sell most of the jewellery items at auction. Andrew donated the handsome amount from the proceeds to the church that Hilary had attended regularly before her passing. He knew the church meant a lot to Hilary and was a haven for her and helped her through many difficult times, especially after Nathan's death.

"Mama Evelyn, please, I'm sure my mother would be very happy for you to have it. I found it when I looked through her box of belongings again the other day. It was her sixtieth birthday gift I bought for her. I don't think she ever wore it."

Andrew handed it back to her. "I won't take no for an answer. Besides, who am I going to pass it on to? It's not like I will be able to wear it." Andrew tried to make a light-hearted joke and squeeze a smile.

"I recognised it right away when I saw the box. Your mother showed it to me once."

The pearl necklace was supposed to be given to Hilary by Andrew during their trip visiting Nathan to celebrate her sixtieth birthday, but they never made it to the USA together, as Nathan died a few months before. Hilary didn't celebrate her birthday that year and never wore the necklace after Andrew gave it to her.

Andrew helped Mama Evelyn put the necklace on; he saw tears in her eyes. There was a bit of an awkward silence for a while; they were both emotional, but for different reasons, and didn't know what to say, which was rare for Mama Evelyn.

Joey came by and asked cautiously, "What's going on? Why are you both so quiet?"

"Nothing, nothing." Evelyn made a hand gesture for Joey to look after the customers.

When Joey walked away to attend to customers, Mama Evelyn said quietly, "Wait here. I want to show you something." She went to her office and came back with two large bags. She showed Andrew the dresses and matching accessories she'd bought for the wedding. She even did a catwalk tour. Mama Evelyn's mood cheered up again.

Andrew joked, "Mama Evelyn, it looks like you are the one who's getting married. Is there something you haven't told me?" They both chuckled. Mama Evelyn put the bags away and came back and sat next to Andrew.

"Last weekend, Joey and I visited Nathan's and your mother's graves. I wanted to tell them that my Sami's getting married. Joey helped me to plant some new flowers around the graves, too."

Her voice grew sad and she hesitated to continue for a few seconds; then she looked at Andrew and said, "I know there were two people who used to visit Nathan's grave tirelessly once a week. One was your mother before she passed away, and the other one was Sami before she moved to Hong Kong. Sami was about ten when Nathan was born, so she was a big part of Nathan's life. She was like a little aunt and big sister to Nathan."

"Mama Evelyn, many thanks for sharing it with me, I really appreciate it; and thank you for planting flowers around the graves." Andrew was really touched, but in order not to upset Mama Evelyn again, he held back his emotions. "I will go there, too, before I leave for Hong Kong." Andrew almost said he'd been to Nathan's grave with Justin a few weeks earlier before coming to the restaurant for dinner, but quickly realised there wasn't any point in mentioning it.

"Good, I'm so happy that we're all going to meet up in Hong Kong. Jimi and Vincent have already left Spain and are now in Thailand." Mama Evelyn sounded very excited. "Wait, don't go yet." Mama Evelyn got up and went to the kitchen to ask the chef to prepare two takeaway bags for Andrew to take home. "You must eat more; you work too much," Mama Evelyn ordered, as she handed over those bags full of takeaway food to Andrew.

About ten days before he departed for Hong Kong, Andrew called Olivia to confirm that he was going to her home to spend the night and that Olivia would drive him to the airport the next morning for his flight. They agreed he should take the train to Glasgow and arrive by late afternoon.

"Looking forward to seeing you again. I'll make a nice dinner. Adrian and I need your advice about renovating our bathroom." As he was about to answer, Olivia asked, "Should I ask Justin to join us, too?"

Andrew's heart went to pieces as soon as he heard Justin's name mentioned. He hadn't heard that name for so many weeks now, and he had thought that he was doing quite well coping in his life without Justin; but apparently not. A strong sense of sadness came over him, before he reminded himself that he needed to answer.

"Oh, it'll be just the three of us. If that is okay? We'll catch up when I see you." After Andrew hung up, he needed a few moments to gather his thoughts.

He said to himself, 'One day at a time. I'll get through this.'

Andrew arrived at Olivia's place just after five p.m. on Saturday. Olivia and Adrian opened the door and before Andrew even stepped inside, they greeted him with a glass of red wine.

"Already?" Andrew took a sip of the wine and nodded his head slightly to let Olivia know he appreciated it.

"We woke up late and started cooking. We had some guests over last night, so drinking seemed to be the most natural remedy for curing a hangover."

They showed Andrew the small bathroom they wanted to refurbish and he gave them some advice and options.

"We want to take out the bathtub, put in a shower with massage function and make more room in the bathroom."

"I can leave you some numbers of tradesmen if you decide to go further with it. But think carefully, as this is the only bath you have in the house. Many buyers would prefer a bath, if you want to sell the house one day."

"Sit in the kitchen and I'll go and find the original floor plan of the house."

Adrian went to his office to find the plans; Olivia and Andrew were alone in the kitchen.

"I need to tell you something." He looked at Olivia. Andrew thought this was a great opportunity.

"As you know, I have spent some time with Justin and he's a really nice guy. My feelings for him have grown, but he doesn't know anything about this. I have decided not to see him for a while, and that was why I thought it might not be a good idea to invite him here tonight. Please don't mention it to him." Andrew was hoping Olivia wasn't able to see through his white lie.

"Wow, that's complicated. I hope you're not getting hurt or anything. Yes, he's a charming guy, but also very much engaged."

Andrew sensed that Olivia didn't sound too surprised by what Andrew had just told her. "I'll be okay. I'll be away for two weeks, which I think will be a good change of scene for me, and I'm hoping for a fresh start when I come back."

"As long as you're all right. Your secret will stay with me, and I won't even share it with Adrian." Olivia gave Andrew a smile. "Here, drink more wine." Olivia refilled his glass almost to the top.

"Thanks. Now, I'm hungry. What are you serving tonight?" Andrew desperately needed to change the subject and was thankful to Olivia that she didn't probe with further questions.

"It's a surprise. I am sure you'll like it. By the way, as you know, Adrian and I have had difficulties trying to get pregnant for a while now, so we're going to start IVF treatment next year. Please don't say anything in front of Adrian. He knew I would tell you, but he's still a bit vulnerable about it." Olivia made a gesture, putting one finger across her mouth as a sign of keeping it a secret. She then called, "Adrian, where are you? Come here, we're about to eat."

About eleven p.m., Andrew became very tired and wasn't able to stop yawning. "Hi guys, thanks for the lovely meal and evening, but I am ready for my beauty sleep." He yawned again. Andrew helped to clear the table and was about to head towards the guest bedroom, where he had slept many times.

Olivia rapidly ran to get in before him. It was almost like she had suddenly thought of something she had forgotten to do. "Wait, don't go in the guest bedroom yet. Let me change the bed linen. I had a few friends over for dinner last night. Justin was here, too, and he stayed over; he left this afternoon," Olivia mumbled, as she went into the guest bedroom.

Andrew helped to change the bed linen and Olivia handed him fresh towels. After a quick shower, he was in bed. Andrew didn't think much of it, but when he lay down it suddenly hit him that Justin had slept in this very same bed the night before. Andrew knew Olivia meant nothing by it, but he wished she hadn't told him so specifically that Justin had been sleeping there in the same bed, having left just a few hours ago.

'How am I supposed to be able to sleep now?' thought Andrew, troubled. He tossed and turned the whole night and wasn't able to sleep, and just as he had fallen asleep, he heard Olivia knocking on the door.

"Andrew, it's time to get up. Get ready and I'll get breakfast for us before I drive you to the airport."

Chapter 15
Please Let Her Live

A few days before Andrew was supposed to return to Scotland, he received a text from Olivia while he was enjoying a Dim sum lunch in a trendy Hong Kong teahouse with Jimi and Vincent.

Hi, Andrew, what exact date/time will you be back? I can pick you up from the airport and take you to the bus station? How was the wedding? Olivia.

Andrew was not expecting this message from Olivia. When Olivia had driven him to Glasgow airport, they had already agreed that he'd take the bus from the airport to Edinburgh. He just wanted to be home as soon as he landed and he could take the bus directly from the airport, which would drive past the main bus station anyway. So he replied:

Hi, Olivia, the wedding was beautiful. I have been eating excellent Hong Kong-style Chinese food every day. I think I must have gained a stone. ☺ You don't need to pick me up. I'll take the bus directly from the airport. Say hello to Adrian for me. Andrew.

A few seconds later, another text arrived from Olivia:

If I remember correctly, you are arriving on a Saturday, so I am off anyway. I just wanted to catch up before you return to Edinburgh. Please let me know your exact arrival date and time and which airline. Olivia.

Andrew didn't know how to turn her down without a good reason. He sent Olivia his exact arrival details and didn't think much of it. He was having a great time visiting different places, and going back to Scotland was not foremost in his mind.

Jimi couldn't remember much about Hong Kong because it was his first time back there since the family immigrated to the UK. It was also Vincent and Andrew's first time there, so the three of them walked a lot and got lost in the many streets, but seeing it as the best way to explore the place.

They loved going to night markets, but none of them were any good at haggling — not even Jimi. He had become too British. They would give Sami a sign that there was something they liked, and then Sami would haggle with the stall owners to get the best price.

They went everywhere. They took the ferry from Hong Kong to Macau, and tried their luck in the casinos. The many grand casinos, the luxury shopping malls and the many rich Mainland Chinese visitors amazed them. They visited Macau's oldest Buddhist temple, A-Ma Temple. They also tried some Portuguese egg tart, Macau's most famous pastry.

The night before Andrew was scheduled to return to Scotland, Sami and her husband invited the whole gang for a seafood dinner. The restaurant was located in a bay area where there were many seafood restaurants. When they arrived, Andrew was surprised that the area and the restaurant was not as fancy as he had imagined, because Sami had told him how special the place was. But the seafood couldn't have been fresher. It had been caught that morning, and some items on the menu were still in water tanks, to be slaughtered just before cooking.

While they were waiting for the chef to prepare the lobster dish, Sami told Andrew, Jimi and Vincent to follow her. "Come with me. I want to show you something." She led them down a small trail towards the water. She stopped and pointed across the water on the other side of the bay. "Do you see those bright lights over the other side? That is China."

The three of them were so shocked at how close it was. Sami told them that from the 1950s to the 1970s hundreds and thousands of people risked their lives and swam from the mainland to Hong Kong; aiming to escape communist rule and in search of a better future. This bay was one of the closest points to China. Many drowned, but for the lucky ones, like Sami's father in-law, this spot was one of the places they first landed when arriving in Hong Kong.

They all fell silent, thinking about the historical significance of the place. Sami was standing between Andrew and Jimi, with Vincent next to him. They all linked arms.

"Do you remember I swore that I'd never get married?" Sami looked at Andrew and Jimi.

"Yes, for a while I thought you were a lesbian," Jimi joked.

Sami had been a tomboy and had always hung around and followed Jimi and Andrew everywhere they went. When she was growing up, she had seen Andrew and Jimi as her two protectors. They were ten years older, but they both adored Sami and cared for her, especially after the divorce of Mr and Mrs Wang, when her dad was almost non-existent and her mother was busy running the restaurant.

Like Joey and Jimi before her, Sami didn't escape her mother's matchmaking arrangements and went on a few blind dates organised on her behalf. But, unlike Joey and Jimi, Sami had always been independent, able to speak her own mind ever since she was a little girl, and was more vocal in protesting to Mama

Evelyn about her dislike of the men and of blind date arrangements.

A year or so after Nathan's death, Sami's family reconnected with Evelyn's relatives in Hong Kong, but only her uncle and his wife and their children, as Mama Evelyn's parents had died many years ago, even before Sami was born.

After university, Sami worked for a few years in Edinburgh and then three years after Nathan's death she moved to Hong Kong and worked for her cousin's import and export business, selling merchandise from China to south-eastern countries.

Her husband's family was in the same line of work and they had met at a business gathering, though she was sure that her mother and her uncle and aunt had had something to do with the set-up. Her husband was only two years older than Sami and had been married once before and then divorced.

Sami took a good look at the three of them and then said, "Listen, we just found out a few weeks ago before the wedding — I'm pregnant." Before the three guys started to burst into a cheer, she waved her hand to stop them and continued, "We haven't told our parents yet, so don't say anything." Once again, she got their attention by waving her right hand in the air. "And, I would like to ask you two to be the godfathers of my child. And, now you can say something." Sami looked at Jimi and Andrew.

Jimi and Vincent were already discussing and arguing about baby names for both a little girl and a little boy. Andrew didn't say a word, but turned around and gave Sami a hug and wouldn't let her go. "It's okay, Andrew. I'm happy to have you in my life, and you'll continue to be in my life through my child." Sami was crying.

"Thank you, Sami. I can't find the words to tell you how happy I am for you and how privileged I am to have you and your family in my life. I'll spoil your child rotten." Not wanting to ruin this happy occasion, Andrew held back his emotions and just continued hugging Sami, letting her know how much he appreciated being a godfather to her child.

"Our turn, our turn!" screamed Jimi and Vincent. The two had a group hug with Sami and asked about the baby's due date. They tried convincing her to give birth in the UK, as Mama Evelyn would be able to give a helping hand with the newborn baby.

"We'll see. I'll have to discuss it with my husband." Sami looked at them. "Seriously, not a word about it."

Before returning to the restaurant, Jimi found a moment alone with Andrew. "How are you doing? Have you heard from Justin? I haven't asked before, as I didn't want to remind you about it."

"I'm fine, thanks; and thanks for asking. No, we haven't been in contact. In a way I was afraid to hear you ask, but at the same time I want to talk about the pain I'm going through. I miss him and think about him constantly. My heart is in pieces."

"Man, sorry I won't be able to get rid of your pain, but if you need someone to talk to, I am here for you. Come and visit us in Spain again. You've only been there once since we moved there. You know, there's always a room for you."

Jimi put his arm around Andrew's shoulder while walking slowly back to the restaurant. Andrew looked back and saw Sami and Vincent behind them, catching up. When they got back to the restaurant, Andrew saw Mama Evelyn looking worried. "Where did you all go?" Mama Evelyn looked at Sami, as she seemed a little angry with her for taking them all out that long.

"Mummy, I showed them the closest point to China from here." Sami tried to calm her down a bit.

"Andrew, sit here next to me." Mama Evelyn pointed at a chair next to her, so Andrew switched seats with Jimi. Suddenly, and for no reason, Andrew became worried that Mama Evelyn was going to ask him something about Justin. Then he thought that was nonsense. He hated that he consumed all his energy thinking about Justin.

Mama Evelyn held one of Andrew's hands. "Thank you for coming all this way for Sami's wedding."

"Mama Evelyn, why do you say that? Of course I wouldn't miss it for the world. I'm so grateful to be here."

"Jimi and Vincent will go with you to the airport tomorrow, and I'll stay on for another week before coming back to Edinburgh. Tomorrow I'll travel to China with Joey and my brother to visit my parents' graves and some old relatives. Both my parents died not long after we moved to Edinburgh, but I was not told at that time, so I missed their funerals. They were buried here first and then my brother moved their ashes back to the old village where our ancestors came from. That was my parents' wish. I'll call you once I'm back. Come over for dinner then."

"Of course, I will come to see you." Andrew nodded his head, assuring Mama Evelyn that he'd keep his promise to come by. Andrew sensed that Mama Evelyn wanted to tell him or ask him something. "Mama Evelyn, is there something on your mind?"

Mama Evelyn quickly looked around and made sure no one was paying too much attention to their conversation. She then lowered her voice. "Can one choose where to be buried in Edinburgh?"

"Why are you asking that?"

Andrew was a bit taken aback and wasn't sure why she had asked this question completely out of the blue. His mind was still occupied with Jimi's question about Justin and the news about Sami's baby.

"Well, Mama Evelyn is asking you a favour. When you're back, could you please check with someone whether there is an available plot in the same cemetery where your mother is buried?" She lowered her voice even further; she didn't want the others to hear what she had just told Andrew.

Andrew glanced at everyone and luckily the others were occupied in a lively and loud discussion about the freshness of the fish and the seafood.

"I can ask. But, Mama Evelyn, you'll live to beyond a hundred." Andrew was joking, but he couldn't picture the day he'd lose Mama Evelyn as well. He didn't know why she had suddenly asked him about the cemetery. 'Is she ill?' Andrew wondered. He didn't dare to ask her directly. 'I will stop by the restaurant when she gets back and have a serious talk with her to find out more.'

He almost wanted to tell her about Sami's baby to cheer her up, but decided it wasn't his place, and he had promised Sami.

"Mama Evelyn, don't worry, I'll do some research once I'm home and…" He was interrupted by a waiter yelling out.

"Be careful, be careful, make space, make space," the waiter shouted, as he put more dishes on the table.

Mama Evelyn pinched Andrew's hand lightly under the table and whispered to him, "No more talk about this. Now, we should enjoy the dinner."

'She does look a bit frail and has lost weight, or am I imagining it?'

Without being too obvious, he took a quick and closer look at Mama Evelyn and pondered the possibilities for the rest of the evening.

Chapter 16
Demons Emerge from Past and Present

After he picked up his luggage, Andrew exited the sliding doors and immediately saw Olivia waving at him. He walked quickly towards her and gave her a hug.

"Welcome back. You must be really tired after the flight." Olivia took one of Andrew's small bags, while Andrew pushed a trolley loaded with two large suitcases.

"I'm actually okay. I slept quite well on the plane. I can't wait to get home for a long hot shower and then bed." Andrew yawned, then burst out laughing with embarrassment. He continued, "You didn't have to come all the way here to get me. I could have taken the bus directly from here to Edinburgh. Wait, I bought something for you and Adrian."

Olivia held his hand tightly to stop him searching for the presents. She led him to a quiet place in the arrival hall and sat him down. Andrew realised that she wanted to talk to him about something. He looked at her in anticipation.

"There's something I need to tell you. Look, I didn't want to worry you when you were in Hong

Kong, but..." Before letting Andrew ask, she continued, "Justin had an accident and is in the hospital. He was critical at first for a few days, but now he's stable. He didn't want me to tell his parents, but Rebecca flew over."

At that point, Andrew just stared at Olivia as she told him about Justin's accident. Andrew could see her lips moving, but he wasn't capable of taking in all the details. However, he was still able to register a few pieces of what she was saying.

"Justin was on his bike and was knocked down when a driver on the inside unexpectedly opened his car door. Due to the speed and the impact, Justin flipped in the air before crashing to the ground. Apart from the bike, which was totally damaged, Justin broke a few ribs, fractured one arm and leg and had a minor concussion, even though he wore a helmet. Luckily, the ambulance and police were called and arrived almost immediately, right after the accident."

Maybe due to jet lag or the fact that he was just so shocked with what she had just told him, Andrew remained calm and not upset, or at least he wasn't allowing himself to be upset. Olivia was worried about Andrew, so she shook his shoulder to check if he was all right; he wasn't reacting.

Like a robot, Andrew stood up and said without emotion, "Please take me to the hospital." On the way there, they were both very quiet. Olivia was crying silently; Andrew just had a blank look on his face, unable to find anything to say.

When they arrived, Olivia led Andrew to the unit where Justin was recovering and pointed to a room along the corridor. "Third room on the left."

Andrew felt his legs become very heavy as he walked towards Justin's room. It was as if all his fatigue and fear had finally caught up with him. As he got closer, his heart began pounding with greater and greater speed. Before he pushed the door open, he took a deep breath and at first looked through the small transparent window in the top right-hand side of the door.

One of Justin's legs and one arm were both in a cast, and he was wearing some sort of protector around his upper body. Andrew took a closer look at him. There he was, a face Andrew had longed to see for so long. Though, at the same time, he almost didn't recognise him; not because Justin's face was covered with bruises, but because when he thought of Justin, he tried not to imagine his face, as it would have been too painful and overwhelming.

Andrew then realised that Justin wasn't alone. A young woman was in the room. 'She must be Rebecca,' thought Andrew.

Since the door was shut, Andrew couldn't hear what they were saying to each other, but got some idea from the way they were interacting. It was like he was watching scenes from a silent movie.

Justin was complaining about the pain and Rebecca was adjusting his pillows to make him more comfortable. Justin was saying something funny and both of them were laughing. Rebecca was feeding Justin yoghurt and they seemed so happy, as a young couple in love should be.

At one point, Rebecca got up and went out of Andrew's sight. Then Justin looked up and he saw Andrew. Andrew stood outside the room and without a word their eyes locked. As if they had just spoken, they both smiled at each other and nodded their heads as if to ask, 'Are you okay?' For a while — it felt like a few seconds only, but also felt like a lifetime — they just looked at each other. Andrew had to stop himself from wanting to open the door, but at that moment he realised that it wasn't just a door that separated them. The door represented the two worlds and the two realities in which they had each chosen to live.

Justin turned his head ever so slightly, looking at the other side of the room, hinting that Rebecca was about to return from the bathroom. At that brief moment before Rebecca came back, it became painfully clear to Andrew that there was no room for him in Justin's life right now. He saw Rebecca come into the room and he walked back towards Olivia.

Olivia drove him home, but Andrew had no recollection of how he got there. He only remembered that he had opened and closed his flat door, dropped his suitcases on the floor and fell onto the bed, falling into a deep sleep.

Andrew was still very tired when he woke up the next morning, even though he had slept through the night. He felt uneasy, as he wasn't sure where he was and what time of day it was. He fell back to sleep again. His head was aching. He was thirsty, but his body was too weak to get up.

On and off he dreamt about Nathan lying in the coffin, the last time he saw his son. Although his face had been 'repaired' by the funeral home staff, Nathan's face somehow appeared to be damaged. It was the image he'd had of Nathan when he had had to identify him in the mortuary.

Andrew dreamt about how he identified Nathan in the morgue and about his funeral. It was almost as if he was watching a slideshow with selected pictures of the event. In his half-asleep stage, some of them became a blur to him and he wasn't sure if some of his memories were correct and exact, or even if they had happened in the sequence that he remembered.

But, deep down, even in his dreams he would always remember the moment he received the call from Mark eleven years ago, informing him of Nathan's accident.

Chapter 17
Bring Him Home

In his dream it was eleven years earlier, mid-February, a cold Wednesday evening around ten p.m. Andrew had just come back from having dinner with his mother at Mama Evelyn's restaurant. He was sitting on the sofa. The TV was on, but Andrew was still contemplating a conversation he had had with his mother.

At dinner he had told her that Nathan was thinking about transferring to a state university and was in the process of applying for a scholarship. She was extremely proud and excited. Andrew told her that once Nathan got into university and settled into his own flat with Olivia, he would take her to visit him in the USA.

"He didn't come home for Christmas. God, I miss him so much. He told me he's found a part-time job delivering takeaways," she said, and Andrew sensed that she wasn't all that thrilled about it. "It's good that he's earning his own money, but I told him not to work too hard and rather to concentrate on his studies. I've never liked him driving in the USA anyway."

Andrew was in his own deep thoughts when at that late hour, his mobile phone rang, making him jump. He saw from the phone screen that it was from Mark, Nathan's host. 'Strange'. Mark had never called him on this phone before. 'Is something wrong?' He turned off the TV and answered quickly.

"Andrew, this is Mark." Andrew recognised his voice right away, as they'd spoken many times via Skype before.

"Hi, Mark. How are you?"

"Fine, thanks. Andrew, I…" Mark appeared to be searching for words.

"Is everything okay?"

"I am very sorry to tell you this. I have some bad news about Nathan."

"What has happened to Nathan? Is he okay?" Andrew's stomach turned.

"Listen, Andrew, I don't know how to say it, but I'm very sorry to tell you that Nathan and Olivia have been in a car accident on the way back from…"

"Are they okay?" Andrew interrupted Mark.

Mark said in a tearful voice, "I'm very sorry, but Nathan was killed."

"No!" Andrew screamed, and, standing up briskly from his chair, he almost lost his balance. His head went blank for a few short seconds and he had to gasp for air. "What happened?" Tears were running down his face.

"Nathan and Olivia drove to the state university for their application interview and on the way back he lost control of his vehicle. It was an icy road and he crashed into the tractor-trailer coming in the opposite direction." Mark paused, as he found it difficult to break the news, but then continued, "Nathan died instantly, due to a fatal brain injury."

At that point, Andrew could feel Mark's pain, even over the phone. "Where is he now?" Andrew asked, his voice echoing in his head.

"After the doctor had declared the cause of death, they moved his body to a mortuary, waiting for his next of kin to identify him and make further arrangements."

"How's Olivia?" Andrew suddenly remembered to ask.

"She was in the passenger seat and was badly injured, with a contusion of the lung and fractured ribs; but she's now in a stable condition. I think her host family have just contacted her family in Scotland, too. I called you first, as I learned from Nathan his mother is on honeymoon."

"Listen, Mark. Many thanks for phoning me. I'm not able to think straight right now. I need a moment. I'll tell Nathan's mother and I'll call you back to tell you about my flight arrangements. I'll try to get the next flight to the USA." Andrew hung up. He really needed some time to himself, to reflect and to figure out what to do next.

His mind went blank and he was in a state of utter shock. He started crying and felt hopeless. Then he stopped, realising that he still had to inform Lena and, worst yet, his own mother. Lena was on honeymoon with her husband. They were in the middle of a cruise somewhere between Europe and Asia. They got married last summer and Nathan attended the wedding, but they had waited till now for their honeymoon.

'How am I supposed to tell her about Nathan's death on her honeymoon?' Andrew decided to wait before calling Lena until he'd made his own travel arrangements.

He picked up the phone and called Jimi in Geneva and told him what had just happened. They both cried and then talked and discussed for a while about various options. Andrew knew he didn't have the heart or strength to tell his mother about Nathan's death, so he asked Jimi to do it. Instead of going with him to the USA, Jimi would go home to Edinburgh to inform Hilary and Mama Evelyn about Nathan and to be with them.

As soon as he ended the conversation with Jimi, the phone rang again, but it was from an unknown UK caller.

"Hello, this is Andrew, who is it?" Andrew wondered, as it was almost midnight.

"My name is Barry, Olivia's father. Olivia's host family phoned earlier and told me about the accident. My condolences for your loss. I met Nathan a few times when he visited us in Glasgow last summer with Olivia. He was a good young man. We were all fond of him."

His use of the past tense angered Andrew, but he nevertheless remembered to constrain himself to have a normal conversation. "Thank you. I've heard that Olivia is hurt, but is now in a stable condition. Do you know more?"

The two searched online to arrange travelling together and were able to book their trips for the next morning to the States. Their flight was to depart from Glasgow, so they agreed to meet at the airport.

Andrew then called Jimi, informing him about his flight itinerary; Jimi told him he was coming to Edinburgh the next day.

"Thanks, man. I owe you one," Andrew cried.

"Don't be silly, brother. I really want to be there for you, but I also know I need to be with your mother. I'll send you a text once I've told your mother, so you can call and talk to her. Don't worry; I'll make sure to take good care of her. I'll stay in Edinburgh as long as it takes." Jimi was crying, too.

Andrew then called Mark and told him his expected arrival time. Mark told Andrew that he would pick him up from the airport and take him to the mortuary.

It was now about two in the morning and Andrew didn't have a clue which time zone Lena was in on her current trip; but as much as Andrew didn't want to, he knew he had to call Lena. 'If the shoe were on the other foot, I would expect to be told right away.'

He called, and Lena answered right away in a very worried voice as she realised something must have gone wrong for Andrew to phone. He asked to speak to Lena's husband first to prepare him. He later told to Jimi that he would remember for as long as he lives Lena's scream and cry when he told her about Nathan's accident. He explained the accident and the cause of his death, as much as he had understood from what Mark told him. He told her that he would fly to the USA in a few hours to arrange the funeral over there. They discussed back and forth whether Lena should also go to the USA, as she wanted to see him for the last time.

"I'll call you as soon as I get there and fill you in on the situation and the procedures." Andrew and Lena were in agreement that Lena should come to the USA, too.

He then remembered he had to pack for his trip, and as he was walking towards the box room to get a suitcase, he passed Nathan's room. He walked in and sat on Nathan's bed. He was in a state of denial. He was totally shut down from his own grief and emotions, as he knew if he were to acknowledge them, he would break down. Suddenly, a sharp pain hit his stomach and he was reminded of what had happened to Nathan. He fell down on the bed. He didn't cry, but a sense of anger, fear and hopelessness was raging inside his head.

In the following few hours there were numerous calls between Mark, Lena and Andrew. At times, Lena called to get more details and clarification. At times she just cried and her words and conversations didn't make any sense; at times Andrew could hear Leif in the background trying to comfort her. There came a point where Andrew was so exhausted and tense that he jumped each time the phone rang.

In the morning, Andrew travelled by bus to Glasgow airport and met up with Barry. They boarded the plane heading for LaGuardia airport, New York, and although they were polite towards each other, neither was feeling particularly talkative through the whole journey; they both had so much on their minds.

While waiting for the next connecting flight to upper state New York, Andrew turned on his phone and saw a few missed calls and text messages from Lena; plus a text message from Jimi.

I am now in Edinburgh. Have you reached your final destination yet? I've talked to your mum. She's devastated, but more worried about you. I will be staying with her for a while. She is home and waiting for your call. Jimi.

On the one hand, Andrew was relieved that his mother now knew about Nathan's death; but on the other hand, he now had to face talking to her. To Andrew, this seemed to be the most difficult phone call he would ever have to make.

Andrew robotically pressed speed-dial for his mother and it was picked up straight away. "Mum, it's Andrew. I'm at LaGuardia airport, waiting for my connecting flight to upper state New York. Are you all right?" Andrew almost wished that Hilary wasn't home or hadn't heard the phone ringing.

"When will you get there and what caused the accident?" Hilary seemed surprisingly calm and composed.

"The next connecting flight will take off in two hours, and Mark, Nathan's host family, will pick me up to take me to the mortuary to identify Nathan and then sign him off to a funeral home." Andrew paused a bit before he continued. His throat was dry; it was almost too painful for him to explain. "On their way back from an interview with the state university, Nathan lost control of his car on an icy road and crashed into a tractor-trailer coming from the opposite direction. Nathan died instantly, due to a fatal brain injury, and Olivia was badly hurt, but is now stable. I'm travelling with Olivia's father."

"Have you spoken to Lena? How is she doing?" Andrew sensed it was Hilary's way of dealing with her pain and grief by asking about others.

"I've spoken to her and I'll contact her again once I've seen Nathan."

"I discussed it with Jimi and he'll come with me to the USA. I want to see Nathan." Hilary was firm in her decision and instructions.

"Mum, let me see Nathan first and I'll let you know our next plan of action. Lena is also waiting to book her flight. Let me talk to Jimi." Andrew felt overwhelmed with all these unknowns and being pulled from different directions.

"Hi, Andrew, don't worry. I'm here with your mum. Keep us posted so we know what steps to take next. Wait, my mum wants to speak to you."

"Andrew! Andrew! Mama Evelyn is so heartbroken. I'm here with your mother. Jimi and I will look after her." Mama Evelyn wept and had to catch her breath from time to time.

"Mama Evelyn, thank you for being there with my mother. I've got to go now, but I'll call again later today." Andrew was unable to continue with the conversation. He didn't know how to handle Mama Evelyn's emotional outburst; he wasn't even ready to face his own loss and grief.

He didn't have the strength left to call Lena, so he sent her a text message letting her know that he had reached LaGuardia airport and was waiting for his connecting flight to upper state New York; he'd call her once he had seen Nathan. He then switched off the phone.

"Are you all right?" Barry asked, handing Andrew a cup of coffee. Barry was worried, as Andrew's face was so pale, as if he was about to faint any second.

"Thanks. I'm fine. There's just so much to deal with." The coffee warmed him and made him feel more alive. "How is Olivia? Have you heard anything?" While waiting for Barry's reply, for a brief second Andrew thought, what if their roles were switched? Then he felt guilty and ashamed to even think that way.

"I just spoke to her family. The doctor is hopeful that she could be transferred out of the intensive care unit soon. She woke up a few times, but is mostly still unconscious; the doctors are optimistic and hopeful that she'll recover in time." Barry slowed down a bit, before he continued, "But they haven't told her about Nathan."

"Oh." Andrew stared at Barry without knowing what to say.

"We're boarding now." Barry pointed at the gate announcement sign.

As they stood up to walk to the queue to board, Andrew felt heavy-footed and wished he didn't have to get on the plane. Suddenly, he was flooded with emotions, and the reality of what was waiting ahead of him hit him hard.

It was a short domestic flight. Before they landed, Andrew looked out of the window to see that it was cold and miserable. He knew there was no turning back and that he had a lot of unpleasant, distressing moments and heartache ahead of him, which he must face. He wasn't sure whether or not he was ready for any of this.

After they had collected their luggage, Andrew and Barry exited the sliding door and were immediately greeted by two men, one of whom Andrew recognised; it was Mark. Andrew quickly assumed that the other man was from Olivia's host family.

One of the men approached Andrew first and took his hand with both of his. "My name is Greg. I'm Olivia's host family. May I offer my condolences for your loss. We've met Nathan many times. He was such a great young man."

For some reason, Andrew was really irritable and thought that maybe he was tired from the trip; then he realised he was irritated with that man for using the past tense to describe Nathan. It was the second time anyone had done so.

'How dare he?' Still, he replied politely, as he knew deep down the man didn't mean any harm.

Andrew turned to look at Mark and shook his hand. Although he'd never met him in person, they had seen each other via Skype many times, especially in the past few months; discussing which car to buy Nathan. It was quite surreal for Andrew meeting Nathan's American host dad in person for the first time, under these circumstances.

"Listen, I'll take Andrew to the mortuary and then to the hotel. We should keep each other informed about any progress," Mark said to Greg and Barry, before leading Andrew towards his parked car.

"I'll take Barry to the hospital to see Olivia." Greg and Barry also headed towards the car park, but not in the same direction.

When they got outside the airport building heading to the parking lot, they were met by freezing cold air, which made it difficult for Andrew to breathe at first.

"Are you warm enough?" Mark realised Andrew was shivering.

"I'm fine, thanks. I will be fine," Andrew answered firmly, as if admitting he was cold would have somehow made Mark think less of Andrew as a father to Nathan.

As the car was leaving the airport, Andrew said to Mark, "I'm very thankful for everything you and your family have done for Nathan, and I'm so sorry you were forced to handle this dreadful situation."

"Don't mention it. My family really enjoyed having Nathan in our lives. He was such a good kid, and everyone enjoyed spending time with him."

As Mark spoke, Andrew still had difficulty adjusting to people using the past tense when talking about Nathan.

Mark continued, "I'll take you to the mortuary to identify Nathan, and then you need to sign a form to release him to a funeral home. My wife's uncle died last year and we used a local funeral home that we were satisfied with. If you don't have any objections, we highly recommend the one we used. I've already spoken to the funeral director."

Andrew nodded and just felt numb as Mark explained all the procedures to him.

"Listen." Mark hesitated a bit, and then said, "I'm very sorry to tell you, but I just want to warn you that Nathan's face was damaged in the accident, but the funeral home should be able to repair it."

Once again, Andrew was unable to find words to describe his feelings and thoughts. His head was filled with questions, fears and dismay.

They arrived at the mortuary and reported to reception, where they were asked to show their identification.

"Go ahead, I'll wait for you here," said Mark. Shortly, a staff member in uniform came over and led Andrew to see Nathan.

They made a number of turns inside the building and then took a lift, one or two floors down. Finally, they were standing outside the room where Nathan's body was being kept.

Before going in, the staff member explained that, in preparation for his visit, they had taken Nathan's body out of the freezer for a few hours. Once the body had been identified, Andrew would have to sign a document releasing it to an assigned funeral home.

"Wait, Mr Hughes, I don't know if you were told, but one side of Nathan's face was slightly damaged in the accident." The staff member looked gently at Andrew and continued, "I'll wait outside. Take as long as you need." He entered the security code and the door opened.

Andrew hesitated for a while and just stood still outside the entrance. His vision became blurred. He took a deep breath and slowly walked in.

It was very quiet in the room; so much so, it was like being in a vacuum. Everything was grey, sterilised and colourless. He felt as if he was in slow motion; everything had stopped and time had frozen. He felt he was having an out-of-body experience. The lights were dimmed and the room was comfortably warm; there was a distinct chemical smell that reminded him of why he was there.

There he was, his son, Nathan, lying on a metal bench, wrapped in a bag with only his face showing. Nathan looked as if he were sleeping peacefully. As Andrew got closer, he saw that one side of his face was noticeably damaged and one of his eyes wasn't closed properly. Andrew saw there were great big welts on his skin, covered in brown dried blood.

Although they had told him that Nathan's body had been taken out of the freezer a few hours before, Andrew still sensed a chill coming from Nathan. He shivered.

Andrew just stood there and looked at Nathan; his mind went blank. He kept looking at him and tried to think of something about Nathan, but wasn't able to. He just stared at Nathan's body and felt nothing. He knew and felt that a part of himself had died along with his son.

Then a voice erupted inside of him. 'I must cry, I must scream, I want to be angry. What kind of father am I?'

He didn't remember much about the rest of the visit. He heard the staff member explaining the procedures to him; he wasn't even sure if he had taken it all in. Andrew robotically signed a few documents and asked Mark to take him back to the hotel, instead of having dinner with Mark's family.

Before Mark drove off, Andrew remembered Mark had told him that he'd pick him up the next morning and go back to the house to collect some clothes for Nathan to wear. They then had an appointment with the funeral director.

Once inside his room, he turned on his phone and there were many missed calls and messages, mostly from Lena; and some from Jimi. He dialled Lena's number and explained quite unemotionally what had just happened and the forthcoming meeting with the funeral director tomorrow. Lena said that she and Leif were getting off at the next port and would try to fly to the USA on the next possible flight.

"Lena, I saw him. I saw Nathan, and one side of his face was hurt. I'm so sorry." Andrew struggled to find the strength to continue, but knew he had to. "I'll meet the funeral director tomorrow and I'll keep you posted." Andrew heard Lena crying and Leif's attempts to comfort her.

After that, he dialled Jimi's number and repeated everything he had just told Lena. He then spoke to his mother, repeating the same thing he had told Lena and Jimi. He was tired and had to stop. He sent one last text message to Lena and turned off the phone.

Surprisingly, he felt hungry and craved a large steak and a beer. Then, without even noticing, he started laughing and thought to himself, 'How can I be hungry and think of food? And I don't even drink beer.'

Out of the blue, he suddenly remembered an interview he had seen on the news a few days earlier. It was about a female TV personality who shed tears after their family pet had died, and she said it was the hardest thing she had ever done in her life when breaking the news to her kids.

His thoughts then came back to his present reality and he said to himself, 'My son has died and I've just seen his body. His beautiful face was damaged and one of his eyes wasn't shut properly.' He began crying hysterically under his pillow, 'He was hurt; my son was hurt.'

The next morning, Mark picked up Andrew and they went to the funeral home that Linda had recommended.

The funeral director, Mr McCarthy, made a professional introduction and welcomed Andrew with a firm handshake. It didn't stop Andrew from feeling uneasy as he entered the funeral home; he recognised that familiar distinctive chemical smell from the mortuary.

'Oh God, the place is stark and bereft of colours, but why are all the colours and decor in here so irritatingly artificial and plastic-looking? The carpet, the lights, the furniture, the walls; and, most of all, even Mr McCarthy!' Andrew felt sick and annoyed after he had a few glances around the place and only a few seconds of meeting Mr McCarthy.

He got even more irritated when Mr McCarthy pointed out something that apparently had already been explained to Andrew, but which he could not recall.

"Mr Hughes, your son Nathan has been transferred to our funeral home. We will restore his face so that he'll look as close as possible to how you remembered him." Mr McCarthy looked at Andrew and Mark. "As he has been released from the mortuary by your admission and to comply with the laws of the State of New York, a decision has to be made within three days of the release of the body; which was last night." He said it as if it was the most natural thing in the world.

"Wait, what do you mean, only three days?" Andrew almost shouted.

"Our sincere apologies if this wasn't explained clearly to you by the mortuary staff. To comply with state law, Nathan will have to be either buried or cremated within seventy-two hours after release from the mortuary, unless you want to transport his coffin back to the UK; then we will need to contact the UK embassy in the USA, which, I believe, is in Washington DC, for special permission, and will require particular procedures." He was softly spoken, but each word was like a nail piercing Andrew's heart.

"But it means Nathan's mother and grandmother might not be able to make it here in time to see him for the very last time!" Andrew started to feel sick and looked to Mark for help.

"Sorry, Andrew, if you hadn't realised this last night at the mortuary; it was explained to you before you signed the release papers. I know you had a lot on your mind." Mark felt really sorry for Andrew and could see Andrew was getting quite pale. "Andrew, do you need to get some fresh air?"

Andrew looked at them both and said, "Sorry, I just need a moment. I'll need to call and talk to Nathan's mother. Please excuse me for a while."

"Take your time. There is a room where you can talk undisturbed. In the meantime, I'll show Mr Harper some coffins." The funeral director got up and showed Andrew the vacant room.

'Take a deep breath, take a deep breath,' Andrew said to himself; he needed to calm down.

Finally, he got the courage to call Lena and tell her about the new developments. It was the first time since Nathan's death that they had argued. Lena was furious, and yelled at Andrew. She then hung up.

Andrew stared at the phone for a few minutes; then it rang. It was Lena. She was still very angry, but they both knew they had to discuss whether Nathan was to be buried or cremated.

"Actually, Lena, I'm not sure it's a good idea for you to see Nathan. His face is damaged; it would break my heart to see you witness it." He needed to tell Lena and protect her.

Lena calmed down and they were able to continue with the discussion. Finally, they both agreed that Nathan should be cremated and Andrew would bring Nathan's ashes to Edinburgh, where they'd be buried.

He knew Lena had a lot of respect for Hilary, and she was grateful to her for bringing up Nathan. Still, it was a relief for Andrew, as he thought Lena would have wanted to bury her son's ashes in Sweden.

"I'll get off at the next port and fly back to Sweden first. I'll wait for your call, letting me know when you'll be back in Edinburgh with Nathan's ashes and when the funeral will take place. I'll wait for you in Edinburgh." Lena was now calm, but detached, as if she had lost all her energy and will to live.

"Lena, I'm so sorry. I'll contact you when I know more."

Andrew waited a bit, as he needed a few minutes to gather his thoughts. He wasn't sure if he had the strength to call Hilary, but he knew he had to and he wanted to, like a little child longing and craving comfort and approval from his mother.

"Andrew? Is that you?" she answered immediately and sounded anxious. Andrew explained to Hilary the procedures and about the decision he and Lena had made.

"I'm so thankful to Lena that she has agreed to the burial of Nathan's ashes here in Edinburgh." As Hilary expressed her gratitude, tears ran down her face. For the first time after learning about Nathan's death, Andrew heard his mother cry.

"Mum, I'll let you know more about the cremation and when I can get his ashes home to Edinburgh. Could you please talk to your church about a service for Nathan and ask Jimi to enquire about a suitable cemetery in Edinburgh?" Andrew was relieved that Hilary would be busy and her mind occupied arranging Nathan's funeral. "Mum, I'm sorry." While talking to his mother, Andrew suddenly felt the wall of detachment between them shatter, and he, too, became tearful and shared his emotions with her.

"Andrew, sorry I can't be there to help. We are here and waiting for you to bring Nathan home." Hilary tried to sound cheerful. "Wait, Jimi wants to say something."

"Hi, Andrew. Don't worry, we'll take care of the arrangements here and wait for you and Nathan."

When Andrew came out of the small office, he felt considerable relief that he and Lena had reached an agreement. As he came out, Mr McCarthy and Mark gave him concerned looks; they must have heard the heated discussion he'd had with Lena.

"Sorry, it took a bit longer than anticipated. May we continue?" Andrew tried to assure them that it was all right to resume their discussion.

Andrew told Mr McCarthy that Nathan's mother had also agreed to proceed with the cremation and to bring Nathan's ashes back to Edinburgh.

Mr McCarthy then showed Andrew a few coffins to choose from that were designed for cremation and informed him that he and Lena would both need to sign a document in order for the cremation to go ahead.

"No problem. I can sign it, then scan it and send it to Nathan's mother to countersign." Then Andrew thought, 'Oh Jesus, how many more papers are there to be signed?'

They discussed organising a wake at the funeral home a few days after on Sunday, so Nathan's friends there could say their final goodbyes. Mark looked at Andrew. "Don't worry about it. My wife and Justin will take care of letting Nathan's friends know."

"Justin?"

"Justin is Nathan's closest friend. They went to the same high school and were studying at the same community college. He lives next door. I'm sure you will recognise him. You must have seen his photos on Nathan's Facebook postings," Mark explained, patiently.

"Oh, okay. I can't remember anything at the moment." Andrew tried for a smile, but failed.

"Mr Hughes, would you like to consider an open or closed casket during the wake? Just to assure you that our funeral cosmetologist and mortician will do their best to make Nathan appear peaceful as if he were sleeping, and create a natural appearance," said Mr McCarthy emotionlessly — yet again. He continued, "Maybe Mark already told you; you will need to bring some of Nathan's clothes so that we can dress him. The sooner the better." He emphasised this last point.

"Let me think about it," Andrew pondered.

Mark jumped in, "I'll take Mr Hughes to my place to choose some clothes for Nathan and then I'll bring them to you this afternoon, at the latest."

"Thank you. That'll make our job a lot easier. I suggest you come back with Mr Hughes once we have prepared and dressed Nathan for the wake. Mr Hughes can then make the decision as to whether the coffin should be open or closed during the wake." Mr McCarthy was trying to make things run smoothly, and it seemed to be working.

Andrew felt a bit calmer. But it was short-lived. He felt uncomfortable again as soon as Mr McCarthy continued listing all the procedures and requirements. "After the wake on Sunday afternoon, we'll transfer Nathan's casket to the crematorium right away. You can pick up Nathan's ashes three days later or maybe even a bit earlier."

Mr McCarthy paused for a few seconds and then continued, "We should also check with the UK Embassy or Consulate about requirements and procedures for entering the UK with his ashes in an urn." Mr McCarthy ran through his checklist and made further requests. Andrew needed to go to the police station to close the case, and then go to the death vital records registrar's office to get a death certificate. In addition, he had to file an application to the court so as to be legally appointed to handle any matters regarding Nathan's estate.

"I really can't think about all the details right now. May I do some research on the internet tonight and get back to you tomorrow?" There was a hint of frustration in Andrew's voice; he wasn't sure for how much longer he could continue making decisions and take in all this new information.

"Mr Hughes, to tell you the truth, many clients have travelled with urns in their hand luggage and Customs officials are often quite lenient and understanding about it. If there are any problems, in addition to the official death certificate, I will also issue you a statement, in case they need to contact me directly," Mr McCarthy tried to reassure Andrew.

Andrew felt short of breath and dizzy. Mark could see Andrew was struggling, so he suggested that they leave and go to the police station later, then come back that afternoon with Nathan's clothes.

As they came out of the funeral home and down the stairs, Andrew stepped on a patch of black ice and almost lost his balance.

"Be careful, Andrew! Are you okay?" asked Mark, managing to grab Andrew's arm so he didn't fall.

"Thanks. I'm fine. And thanks for getting me out of there. I wasn't sure how much I could take in any more." The cold air cleared his head. "I'm so grateful to you and your wife for all your help," he said. "I'm so sorry to have put you through this."

"Really, don't mention it. Linda and I were very fond of Nathan and he'll always remain a part of our family," said Mark tenderly. "I think we should have lunch, so you'll have a bit of breathing space before we go home and get Nathan's clothes."

They had lunch in a diner nearby and Andrew regained a bit of strength. There was a burning question on his mind that he was afraid to ask, but knew he had to. "How exactly did the accident happen?"

Mark became emotional as he described the accident. "Nathan and Olivia drove to the state university for their interviews. It was very cold and the roads were slippery due to black ice. Based on witness accounts and the police report, Nathan's car suddenly spun round three times and he lost control, crashing into a large truck coming in the opposite direction. Based on the police investigation, Nathan must have become concerned when he saw a large truck coming towards them and hit the brakes too hard, causing the car to spin. It happened so suddenly that the truck driver didn't have time to react and didn't have enough space to manoeuvre."

Andrew listened, as if it were a story about someone else; he was just so shocked and overwhelmed by Mark's account of the events. They both sat there in silence. Then Mark looked at Andrew. "You must have a lot to think about right now, but Linda and I will do our best to support you in any way."

"Once again, my family and I are so grateful to you for all your help. I really don't know what I would have done without your support," Andrew thanked them sincerely.

Mark called Linda, telling her that he was coming home with Andrew to get Nathan's clothes and about the wake in two days' time. "Linda and Justin will set up a post on a Facebook page about the wake so that Nathan's friends can be informed. Technology, huh?" Mark tried to ease the mood a bit.

When they entered the house, Linda embraced Mark and then Andrew. She hugged him so tight; she thought it was a way to express her compassion.

They sat down and Mark explained to Linda all the arrangements and that they'd have to go back to the funeral home with Nathan's clothes. Linda confirmed that the announcement about the wake had been posted. Andrew sat there, listening to their conversation; he felt so tired, and everything was beginning to catch up with him. "Andrew, are you okay? Can I get you something to drink?" Linda could see that Andrew was struggling to keep his eyes open.

The sensation of fatigue came and went swiftly. Suddenly, Andrew realised where he was and what he was there for. "Oh, here are two bottles of fine Scottish whisky I bought for you, and also a few toys I bought in the airport for your two kids. My family and I are forever grateful for what you have done for Nathan." Andrew handed over the two bags to Linda.

"You didn't have to do that, but thank you very much; that was very thoughtful. Nathan will remain part of our family. My two children are now with my parents. I sent them there for a few days, but they'll be attending the wake to say their final goodbye to their big brother." Linda had tears in her eyes.

To change the subject, Mark said, "Can I show you Nathan's room? You can choose some clothes for Nathan to wear." Andrew followed Mark to the second floor of the house. "That's Nathan's room. Linda and I will be downstairs; take your time."

Andrew opened the door and entered the room. Straight away, he recognised some of Nathan's belongings and clothes. On his desk was a picture of Lena and her children; there was one of Hilary and a photo of Andrew and Nathan that Jimi had taken when they were in Geneva just a few months ago.

Andrew then looked inside a cupboard and took out a few of Nathan's clothes. Andrew saw the whole dinner jacket and black-tie outfit Lena had bought for Nathan to wear at her wedding a few months ago. He folded the outfit into a bag to take to the funeral home for Nathan to wear.

He sat on the bed for a few minutes and sobbed. He covered his face with Nathan's clothes, trying to stifle the sound he was making, but this made him cry even harder; he could smell Nathan. Then he recognised the quilt spread out on the bed. Originally, it was a small comfort blanket Hilary had made for Nathan when he was born.

Although Nathan had bonded well with Hilary when Lena first went back to Sweden, he cried incessantly for days. Maybe subconsciously or unconsciously, although Nathan was just a few months old, he sensed his mother was not with him. Hilary, Mama Evelyn and Andrew had tried all they could to comfort Nathan and to make him stop crying. Hilary then made a small comfort blanket for Nathan and the colourful and bright patterns with cute animals had caught Nathan's attention and were able to calm him down. Ever since, he seldom parted with it.

Throughout the years, the comfort blanket had been washed, torn, stitched and repaired and enlarged to a quilt. Andrew knew how much the comfort blanket and later the quilt meant to Nathan. Andrew folded the quilt and put it inside the bag, along with the dinner jacket, tie, a shirt and underwear.

That afternoon, Mark drove Andrew back to the funeral home with Nathan's clothes. He was told to come back the next day in the early afternoon, when Andrew would have to decide whether to have an open or closed casket at the wake.

Mark and Linda had invited Andrew to stay over for dinner that evening, but Andrew was utterly exhausted, so Mark just dropped him off at his hotel. "I'll pick you up tomorrow around two p.m.!"

"Once again, many thanks; my regards to Linda. I'll see you tomorrow afternoon." Andrew waved as Mark drove off. He was tired and worn out, but he knew he had to call Lena and his mother to let them know about the wake and about Nathan's ashes. 'I'll see Nathan again tomorrow and then I'll make a decision about whether or not to have an open casket at the wake. I should be able to leave here on Thursday and be home by Friday next week.'

Jimi told Andrew that they'd found a cemetery to place Nathan's urn the next Sunday; there would be a service for him at Hilary and Mama Evelyn's church in Edinburgh.

The next afternoon, Mark picked up Andrew and they headed for the funeral home. "Andrew, are you okay?" Mark asked, sensing Andrew's unease.

"I'm a bit nervous about what they've done to Nathan's face."

"I can understand your concern. I'm sure the funeral cosmetologist and mortician will have done their best to restore Nathan's face," said Mark, trying to comfort Andrew.

Mark sat in the waiting room, allowing Andrew to see Nathan on his own. Andrew entered the large reception room where the wake was to take place the following afternoon.

'There he is! My son.' Nathan was lying in a coffin, nicely dressed in the dinner jacket Lena had bought him. The funeral cosmetologist had done a good job. Nathan looked almost unhurt and less waxy than Andrew had feared. His face was mostly restored. He looked natural, handsome and peaceful, like he was sleeping. Andrew was relieved, and his heart filled with gratitude. Without knowing, he had a hint of a smile on his face.

About twenty minutes later, Mr McCarthy and Mark entered the room and discussed with Andrew the details of tomorrow's wake. Andrew had finally decided, it would be an open casket. Mark left around four p.m. and would be back later with Linda. Andrew closed the room door and was alone again with Nathan.

He sat on the chair, looking at the casket in front of him where Nathan was lying. So many memories about Nathan's birth and childhood came to him. He was so grateful to have had Nathan in his life, and he had touched the lives of so many people; he was loved by many.

He took out his phone, called Lena and told her where he was. He said he was so pleased with the work they had done on Nathan's face. "May I speak to Nathan?" cried Lena.

Andrew placed his mobile phone next to Nathan's ear so Lena, Nathan's half-siblings, Lena's parents and Leif could say their final goodbyes.

"Andrew, thank you for all you've done. I'll see you in Edinburgh next week. I have spoken to your Mum as well." Lena was somewhat at peace.

Andrew then dialled his mum's number; Mama Evelyn, Jimi and Sami were all at her place. He did the same, placed his phone near Nathan's ear. Andrew wept as he listened to their heart-breaking farewells to Nathan.

Mark and Linda came back to the funeral home around seven p.m. and Andrew left them alone with Nathan.

That evening, they went out for dinner. It was the first time Andrew had eaten anything decent since receiving the news about Nathan's death. He slept that night.

On the day of the wake, Mark and Linda came to the hotel where Andrew was staying. They stopped first at a flower shop to pick up some flowers, before driving to the funeral home. They arrived about one hour earlier than the announced time, just so Andrew, Mark and Linda were able to be sure that everything was organised.

As Linda and Mark were discussing some final details with Mr McCarthy and the staff of the funeral home, Andrew went in the room where the wake would take place. Although Andrew had already seen Nathan the previous day, it still made Andrew's heart ache to see Nathan lying in the coffin. 'How am I supposed to bury my own son?' Andrew wondered, his mind conflicted with thoughts of the reality of what was happening in front of him and the inconceivableness of the situation.

Suddenly, he heard children's voices. They were Mark and Linda's two children. They came with Linda's parents. This was the first time he had met Mark and Linda's children. "This is Nathan's father." Linda let go of their hands and pushed them forward a bit towards Andrew while introducing them to him. "Jacob is six and Alice is eight."

Andrew crouched down to their eye level. Natural and not shy at all, they just ran up to Andrew and gave him a hug so tight that it got Andrew emotional right away.

"Can we see Nathan?" They asked for chairs to stand on. As soon as they got up and saw Nathan, without any hesitation or fear they started tenderly touching Nathan's face and holding Nathan's hands with their small hands. Surprisingly, they did not cry, nor were they scared. They were talking to Nathan with overwhelming affection just as if he was still alive.

Mark, Linda and Andrew didn't say a word. They stood quietly with tears in their eyes, watching them talking and saying goodbye to their big brother Nathan.

The children left with Linda's parents before the wake started. Andrew spent some time in the toilet to compose himself before everyone arrived. He closed his eyes for a moment and splashed cold water on his face. He opened his eyes and looked at his own image in the mirror. 'Nathan, I will get through it. Please be with me.'

Andrew didn't recognise anyone except Nathan's host family and Barry. But he was hugely taken aback by how many people attended the wake; Andrew was proud and touched. Andrew took some pictures during the wake and sent them to Lena and Jimi.

Barry came to the wake and updated Andrew on Olivia's condition. She was recovering, but was devastated to hear about Nathan's death. Barry and Olivia would be heading back to Glasgow once Olivia had recovered well enough to travel.

He met Justin for the first time. Linda introduced Justin to him as Nathan and Olivia's best friend living next door to Linda and Mark's. Andrew didn't pay any special attention to Justin, as there were so many people to greet. He did, however, remember thanking Justin for being Nathan's friend and for his help posting notices on Facebook about the wake.

After the wake, when everyone had left, with the help of the funeral staff home, Andrew gathered the flowers and cards people had brought. His mind was occupied when flicking through the memory book signed and written in by the guests who had attended.

Andrew told Mr McCarthy that he needed time alone with Nathan. It broke his heart, as he knew the coffin would be transferred to the crematorium later that same day.

Andrew closed the door. All went quiet. Finally, Andrew was alone with Nathan again.

Andrew took a chair and sat in front of Nathan's coffin, reading notes and stories people had written in the memory book. As he read some of the nice things people had written about Nathan, with tears in his eyes, Andrew smiled.

He closed his eyes for a minute and then looked at Nathan. "My dear son, how is it possible for me to say goodbye to you. Arranging your funeral and burying you is and will be the hardest thing I have to do in my life." Tears ran down his face unstoppably as he stroked Nathan's face ever so gently. He wished he were the one laying inside the coffin instead of Nathan.

Andrew placed photos of Hilary, Lena, Nathan's half-siblings and himself inside the coffin. Andrew then covered Nathan with the quilt that Hilary had made for him when he was little. Seeing Nathan dressed in the dinner jacket and covered with the quilt provided profound comfort to Andrew, as he knew they were embedded with love, protection and strong bonds between Nathan, his mum and his grandmother. Andrew tucked Nathan in for the very last time.

"Son, don't be afraid. I will bring your ashes home to Edinburgh. Your mother, grandmother, Mama Evelyn, Uncle Jimi and Sami will all be waiting for you back there," Andrew firmly whispered his promise to Nathan.

Someone knocked gently on the door. It was Mr McCarthy, politely reminding him about the time. Andrew took a last look at Nathan's face, trying to capture and absorb that moment. He didn't want to leave Nathan, but he knew he had to. "Wait for me, my son. One day we will meet again."

In the days that followed, Andrew helped Mark and Linda to clear Nathan's room. He found the watch Jimi had bought Nathan for his graduation when they were in Geneva about six months ago. It looked as if Nathan had never worn it. With Jimi's permission, Andrew gave it to Mark as a token of gratitude for all his help.

Andrew packed some of Nathan's clothes and belongings to bring them home to Scotland for Lena and Hilary.

Three days after the wake, Mark picked up Andrew to take him to the crematorium. A staff member handed Andrew a small cardboard box containing Nathan's ashes. When Andrew held it in his hands, it was heavier than he had anticipated. He felt a sense of closeness to Nathan. He held Nathan's ashes all the way back to the funeral home; it was almost like holding Nathan for the first time in his arms when he was born.

In the afternoon of that same day, Andrew saw Mr McCarthy for the last time and picked up the urn and settled the bills. Mr McCarthy handed Andrew a few documents and certificates and reassured him that everything would be all right. Although Andrew knew no one could have the power and authority to make any guarantees, it still felt good to hear those words. Mark took copies of all bills and certificates to be sent to the insurance company on behalf of Andrew.

It was time for Andrew to return to Glasgow. He invited Mark, Linda and her parents out for dinner. He had grown so close to this family, and without their help he would have been unable to cope. A few years later, Mark, Linda and the kids actually came to visit Andrew in Edinburgh as part of their tour of Europe.

Andrew had an official statement from Mr McCarthy and the crematorium, plus, a death certificate issued by the State of New York. Still, Andrew was very nervous, particularly the night before his flight. He was afraid that Customs officials would stop him

271

from bringing Nathan's ashes to the UK. He hardly had any sleep during the whole flight back to Glasgow, as he was feeling unsettled and worried about any potential questions and complications with the authorities. Losing a son was bad enough; Andrew couldn't face being interrogated at the airport.

He arrived at Glasgow airport, and before exiting Customs, he held his small piece of hand luggage with Nathan's ashes inside tightly and close to his chest. He closed his eyes and communicated to Nathan, 'Nathan, your mother, your grandmother and lots of people who love you are waiting for you outside. Please help me through Customs without any problems. I've done everything I can; now it is your turn to help me.'

He took a deep breath and exited Customs. He saw his mum, Lena, her family, Jimi, Mama Evelyn and Sami.

"Nathan, you're home!" Andrew whispered.

Chapter 18
Unknown

Ding. Ding. Ding. Ding.

Andrew was woken by the sound of the doorbell, someone knocking and banging on the door and the faint sound of someone calling out his name. "Andrew! Are you home?"

'What's happening? What time is it?' Andrew then realised his whole body was in pain.

"I'm coming!" he shouted. His throat hurt. He got up with the sense that every bone of his body ached. He put on a morning robe and walked in confusion towards the door. "I'm coming." He opened the door and was surprised to see Joey. 'Why does he look worried? Why is he here?'

"Thank God you are home and you're all right. We've been back for two days. My mother has been calling you loads of times since yesterday and she's worried 'cause you haven't answered."

Slowly, Andrew recalled what happened. Ever since he got home from Hong Kong, he had been working non-stop. With the combination of fatigue, jet lag from the trip and the emotional drain from seeing Justin in the hospital, his body just broke down and he had caught flu.

"Oh, hi, Joey. I'm sorry I haven't answered my phone. I turned it off. I had a temperature and flu, so my GP put me on antibiotics. I've been in bed for the last few days."

"My mother's been worried. She sent me here. I rang your building entrance doorbell and you didn't answer. Luckily, one of your neighbours recognised me from the restaurant and let me in, after I explained to her I was looking for you. Are you okay? You look very ill."

"Thanks. I'm getting better now. A few days ago, I could hardly move or talk. Do you want to come in and can I make you some tea?" Andrew realised his throat was dry and still hurt and he needed to drink some water.

"No, thanks. I'm going now. Stop by the restaurant to see my mother when you're feeling better." As Joey was heading towards the lift, he suddenly stopped and turned back. "Have you eaten? Do you need food shopping or should I come back with some food from the restaurant?"

"Oh. No. Thanks." Andrew pictured Mama Evelyn coming by with tons of Chinese home remedy medicines and lots of food. "Joey, please tell your mum that I'm better now and I'm on antibiotics and I should be on my feet in a few days. I will come by to see her. Please don't let her bring me any home remedies or food."

"You know my mother well." Joey smiled as he said goodbye to Andrew, before heading to the lift.

Andrew dragged himself to the kitchen. He must have drunk two large glasses of water one after the other. He walked slowly back to his bedroom. He sat on the bed and took the antibiotics as he turned on his phone. He took a look at it and saw it was after three in the afternoon. There were some Messenger messages from Jimi. He had sent Andrew pictures of his and Vincent's tour in Asia. He had a smile on his face when he saw some of the photos Jimi had sent, but he was too tired and weak to reply. Then, there were about ten missed calls, mostly from Mama Evelyn. He put the phone on silent and as soon as his head hit the pillow he was gone again.

Andrew dreamt about Nathan again and he dreamt about Justin. At times, Justin was killed in a car accident instead of Nathan. At times, Nathan's face was covered in bandages. He also dreamt that he was lying in a coffin, but he was alive. Someone was about to shut the cover of the coffin, so he screamed, "Help! Don't close the cover! I am inside!" He shouted, but no one seemed to be able to hear him.

Andrew tossed and turned and was in and out of sleep. Finally, he woke up. It was the next morning. His fever was gone, but his bed covers were soaked with sweat. Andrew was still a bit dizzy and weak, especially after the weird and draining dreams he had had, but somehow, he felt much better. His throat wasn't hurting as much and his bones were not as badly sore as they had been for the past few days.

He took a long shower and got dressed. His stomach made a rumbling sound, which reminded him he was hungry. He remembered getting up a few times through the night to use the bathroom and take the antibiotics, but he didn't remember eating anything.

He went to the kitchen and prepared an omelette on toast and already felt much more alive with the smell of brewed coffee. After he had had his breakfast and probably the first real meal he had had for days, he felt he was himself again. 'Oh gosh, how long had I been sleeping? I must have been in and out of sleep for three days.' The last thing Andrew remembered was collapsing in bed when he got home from the GP last Friday. 'Wow, I must have been sleeping for three days,' he thought.

As he was changing his bed sheets, he thought to himself, 'I must call or go and visit Mama Evelyn this afternoon. She must have been worried sick about me.' Andrew was also puzzled about the conversation he and Mama Evelyn had had the last night he was in Hong Kong. 'I hope she is not ill.'

"Andrew. How are you? I have been waiting for your call." Mama Evelyn must have waited anxiously for Andrew's call; she answered it straight away once the phone rang.

"I'm fine, thanks. I had the flu for about a week and now I'm feeling much better." It warmed Andrew's heart to hear Mama Evelyn's energetic voice.

"I have been worried. Joey forbade me to call you again so as not to disturb you while you were ill," Mama Evelyn complained.

"Mama Evelyn, you don't disturb me at all." Andrew had a smile on his face, imagining the conversation between Joey and his mother.

"Do you need me to bring you food or medicine?"

"No, Mama Evelyn, I am fine now. Please don't bring anything," Andrew said in an assertive voice to make sure she really understood.

"Okay, no medicine. Andrew, I need to talk to you. May I come by your place?" He could hear the sense of urgency in her request.

"Of course. Come any time this afternoon. Is there something the matter? Are you all right?" Andrew looked at his computer, which indicated two p.m., and his calendar to make sure he had no meetings or teleconferences booked, as he didn't want to be disturbed while spending time with Mama

Evelyn. He was anxious to find out whether something was wrong.

"I will come around three p.m. Mama Evelyn needs to ask you for a favour. I will bring you something you like."

"Mama Evelyn, really, there's no need to bring anything. Ask me anything; I would be happy to help," Andrew insisted again.

Andrew was anxious while waiting for Mama Evelyn. He thought about the conversation they had had in Hong Kong. He had been worried ever since, and was even more so, now that Mama Evelyn had specifically asked to visit him alone in the flat. 'What she wants to talk to me about must be something she does not want Joey to hear. I hope she is all right.'

The doorbell rang. Andrew pressed the intercom buzzer and it was Mama Evelyn. "Andrew, I am here. Come down. I need your help with carrying bags." Mama Evelyn sounded breathless over the speakerphone.

"I'm coming, Mama Evelyn!" As he took the lift down, he thought, 'What in the world did she bring?' As soon as he opened the entrance door to his building, he recognised the restaurant takeaway delivery guy, Chris, carrying bags out from his car next to the entrance. Andrew said hello to Chris and went to help. "Mama Evelyn, what are all these?"

"Nothing. Just some food." Mama Evelyn said goodbye to Chris and counted the bags to make sure they were all there. Andrew carried them all up in the lift and then put them on the kitchen table. He looked at Mama Evelyn, who seemed excited and had the semblance of a child who had done something naughty.

"Mama Evelyn, did you bring the whole supermarket with you?" Andrew joked, and looked at Mama Evelyn, who was unpacking and instructing what to put where. Andrew gasped, seeing so many items, including, dishes packed in takeaway containers from her restaurants, fresh meat, fresh fish, vegetables, hams, fruits, cookies, bread, cakes, a box of tea bags, a jar of coffee and some over-the-counter cold and fever medications.

"Mama Evelyn, you didn't have to bring all this food! I won't be able to eat it all." Andrew was amazed.

"Don't worry. You can freeze most of it."

"What are these?" Andrew saw a large stack of paper napkins he recognised from her restaurant and a bottle of hand-wash soap.

Mama Evelyn giggled. "I must have put them in one of the bags when I was in a hurry to get in the car. It's always good to have paper napkins at home. The restaurant ordered extra for this year's Fringe

Festival." Mama Evelyn had a good explanation for everything, and was pleased with her own logic.

After they spent some time putting everything away in kitchen cupboards and some in the fridge and some in the freezer, Andrew asked, "Mama Evelyn, do you want something to drink? Should I make Chinese tea?"

"Okay. Chinese tea. Put the tea leaves in the cup." Mama Evelyn never used tea strainers when drinking Chinese tea. As Andrew was making tea, he said to her, "Mama Evelyn, please go and sit on the sofa in the living room; it's more comfortable there."

When he came in with the tea, Mama Evelyn was sitting comfortably on the sofa, but looked a bit unease.

"Mama Evelyn, tell me. What is the matter?" Andrew asked. He sat opposite, looking at her gently.

"Andrew, I have known you since you were little and really feel that I can share this with you, as Sami and Jimi are far away and Joey is still troubled finding a new life since the divorce. I hope you don't mind me bothering you with this." Mama Evelyn almost had tears in her eyes.

Andrew didn't like the sound of her preface. "Mama Evelyn. Don't worry. Thanks for trusting me with it. Whatever it is, we can sort it out." Now Andrew was really worried, but he gave Mama Evelyn a reassuring look.

"Okay." Mama Evelyn sat up straight. "For years I have been receiving a bowel screening kit for testing and I never paid attention to it." She paused to find the words. "Before travelling to Hong Kong, I heard the ladies in the bridge club talking about it and discussing some of the symptoms, and it frightened me." From her handbag, Mama Evelyn took out the instructions and kit for testing she had received and handed them over to Andrew.

"Why did it worry you? Did you notice some of the symptoms?" Andrew asked, at the same time as he was reading the instructions.

"I…" Mama Evelyn hesitated and did not look at Andrew.

"Mama Evelyn, don't be embarrassed." Andrew was trying to give her encouragement, but was also slightly cautious as he sensed she was very uncomfortable about it. He waited for her to take her time.

"Ever since before travelling to Hong Kong, periodically I experienced severe pain in my stomach that won't go away and I also have blood when I go to the toilet." Her voice became lower and lower as she finished her sentence.

Andrew had seldom seen Mama Evelyn look so shaky. Although Andrew was alarmed by what she had told him, he didn't want to put his worries on top of Mama Evelyn's. "Mama Evelyn, don't worry.

We'll figure it out together. How are you feeling now?"

"I feel better now, but the problem still occurs from time to time. You know what I mean?" Mama Evelyn sounded frustrated and deflated.

Andrew read the instructions for the testing kit thoroughly, while Mama Evelyn waited in anticipation. He then patiently showed the different parts of the kit to Mama Evelyn and explained to her carefully, "Mama Evelyn, you need to take samples for five days, twice a day, within a ten-day period." He showed her how to collect the samples using the cardboard sticks provided. "Here is how you put your name sticker on and this is how you open and close the sample windows for each day."

In order to be sure that she really understood, he asked Mama Evelyn to show him how she would do it. They practised a few times till Andrew was convinced she would know what to do.

"We should also make an appointment with your GP while waiting for the results. What is the phone number of your GP?" He dialled the number Mama Evelyn gave him and made an appointment for three and half weeks' time. "Hopefully, we will have received the test results by then." He looked at Mama Evelyn, who now seemed relieved as Andrew took over all the arrangements.

"Andrew, I am so grateful you are doing this for me." Her voice cracked and tears ran down her face. It worried Andrew a bit, as he had never witnessed Mama Evelyn so frightened and deflated before.

"Mama Evelyn, of course I would do anything to help. Don't worry, whatever happens, I will be here for you." He reached over and gave her a tissue and patted her on the back to comfort her.

"Don't tell Sami or Jimi yet. I will tell them once we know more."

"Mama Evelyn, of course I won't say anything to them till you are ready. Oh, your tea must be cold." Andrew got up, heading to the kitchen to make more tea.

"No more tea. I am going back to the restaurant." Mama Evelyn stood up and walked towards the door.

"Mama Evelyn, don't you want to stay for dinner? You brought so much food. I can easily warm up some of it?" Andrew held her hand and led her to the kitchen.

"Oh, thank you, but I need to go back to the restaurant now. Joey knows I am here visiting you, but he will start to worry, as I have been away for a few hours and the busy time starts soon," Mama Evelyn insisted.

"I will take you back to the restaurant." Andrew put on his shoes, as he knew there was no point arguing with Mama Evelyn.

"No need, no need. I know my way. I will take the bus back." Mama Evelyn waved her bus pass.

"Mama Evelyn, don't be silly. I'll call a taxi and I will come with you. Besides, I can get some fresh air walking home after I have dropped you off. I'll need all the exercise I can get in order not to put on weight with all the food you brought." As Andrew smiled at Mama Evelyn, he opened the door and led her to the lift. While waiting for the taxi, Andrew said to her, "Call me each day after you have collected the samples and come by when all the samples are taken and I will send them off for you."

"Oh, Andrew, thank you."

"Mama Evelyn, don't worry. I am here for you…"

"I will be all right. Besides, I am not ready to go just yet. Sami told me you knew about her pregnancy as well." Mama Evelyn's face lit up, but only briefly, before her voice saddened. "When Joey's two boys were born, they already lived in Newcastle, so I didn't see them as much as I had hoped. Since the divorce, Joey's ex-wife hasn't made much of an effort to make opportunities for me to spend time with them, either. They are, of course, adults now, but sadly the bond isn't there."

"Yes, Mama Evelyn, you will be a grandmother again. I am sure Sami would love you to be a hands-on grandmother." Andrew smiled.

"Did you investigate finding me a place in the same graveyard as your mother? I…"

Mama Evelyn was interrupted by Andrew. "Mama Evelyn, don't worry. Let's do the tests first and see what they tell us. Oh, our taxi is here!" He opened the taxi door for Mama Evelyn.

In the following days, Mama Evelyn made quick calls to provide Andrew with updates about her progress with the sample-taking. It was almost as if she was a proud student reporting back to her teacher.

"Andrew, I have finished. I have finished the samples." Mama Evelyn said it over the phone with great satisfaction.

"I will come to the restaurant this afternoon so we can send off the test kit."

"I don't want you to take time off from your work. I am playing bridge tonight, so I can come to your flat before that. Around six p.m.?"

When Mama Evelyn arrived at Andrew's place, she stood in the entrance, and before she had even taken her shoes off, she impatiently handed him a sizeable parcel wrapped in layers and layers of newspaper.

"What is this?" Andrew was puzzled.

"The sample kit. I was afraid there might be a bad smell, so I wrapped the kit in newspaper," Mama Evelyn explained proudly.

"Mama Evelyn, there shouldn't be any bad smell from it. Come in. Where is the return envelope?" Andrew unwrapped the parcel and found the small sample kit. "You scared me a bit," he smiled.

"I am just here to drop this off. I am going to my bridge evening now. Have I given you everything?"

"Yes. Let me double-check." Andrew looked to make sure everything had been included and slipped the thin sample kit inside the small return envelope.

"Thanks. I am off now. I will put it in the post on my way to bridge." Mama Evelyn took the envelope from Andrew's hand.

"Wow, Mama Evelyn, you are dressed as if you are going on a date. Anything I should know?" Andrew chuckled as he opened the door for her.

"This is no time to joke about your old Mama Evelyn," she laughed.

"Enjoy your bridge night. Contact me when you get the results or if you are not feeling better."

Mama Evelyn went into the lift and waved both of her hands to Andrew as the doors closed.

A letter from the NHS came around two weeks after Mama Evelyn had sent off the test kit. Mama Evelyn came straight to Andrew's place as soon as she received it.

"Open and read it for me, please, Andrew. I am too scared to do it myself." Mama Evelyn nervously handed him the letter.

"Mama Evelyn, I am so pleased for you that your test result shows that there are no traces of blood in your bowel motion." Andrew read the results letter carefully and announced the result joyfully to Mama Evelyn, as she waited anxiously.

"Oh, I feel so relieved, but at the same time I wonder why I am still experiencing those symptoms sometimes?" Mama Evelyn looked happy, but still a little concerned.

"Mama Evelyn, don't worry. We will see your GP in a few days." Andrew gently patted Mama Evelyn's back to comfort her.

A few days later, Andrew accompanied Mama Evelyn to visit her GP and was told that, though the test would pick up the majority of bowel cancers, it was not one hundred per cent accurate, especially given Mama Evelyn's age and the symptoms she had been experiencing.

"However, I don't want to worry you, because the symptoms you described can also be caused by other health issues, not necessarily bowel cancer." Her doctor patiently explained it to them while taking blood samples from Mama Evelyn.

"It is better to be sure. In addition to this blood sample, I will also refer you to the hospital for other tests," continued the handsome doctor. With a quick glance, Andrew had seen a ring on the GP's finger. 'What a shame, he is married. Wait. Behave!'

Andrew secretly had a smile on his face, but was surprised at himself for thinking about the doctor in that way at that moment, and managed instead to concentrate on his report on Mama Evelyn.

"Mama Evelyn, please let me know when you have received the blood test results and the hospital notification about the other tests referred by your GP." Andrew walked Mama Evelyn back to the restaurant, because she wanted to have some fresh air after the visit to the GP.

"Andrew, thank you for coming along. I will call you when I have the results and notice about the hospital appointment." Mama Evelyn certainly looked less worried, but still concerned about the uncertainty and about the other tests she was told to take.

"Mama Evelyn. Don't mention it. Do you want to tell Joey, Jimi and Sami now? I communicate with Jimi and Sami through Facebook and Messenger, but I haven't said anything about it."

"I guess so. I will talk to them." Mama Evelyn sighed and slightly nodded her head.

Chapter 19
Turning the Page

Ever since Olivia had picked Andrew up from the airport after he had arrived from Hong Kong and they had gone to visit Justin in the hospital, she had only had a few brief text message exchanges with Andrew. At times she felt guilty for having reintroduced Justin into Andrew's life.

Although she was happily married to Adrian, she thought about Nathan and missed him often, and the scars from the car accident on her body reminded her of him, as if she could ever forget or erase it, even if she wanted to. She remembered vividly how she had screamed when they told her about Nathan's death. In a strange and selfish way, since the visit to the hospital, she was secretly happy to think that what had developed between Andrew and Justin was more than just a friendship; somehow in her mind it would have preserved Nathan's legacy.

Andrew, on the other hand, had been busy and tied up with Mama Evelyn's tests and hospital visit arrangements for other tests. He also drowned himself in work, sorting out new rental contracts, and one of his buy-to-let flats had a burst pipe in the bathroom, causing a water leak into the flat below. Deep down, he knew that the reason he kept himself busy and was avoiding Olivia was mainly because it would have been too painful for him to either think or to forget about Justin. Olivia was the only person connecting him and Justin, and the less he learnt about Justin the better.

Olivia wasn't overly sensitive, but she was not dumb, either. She could sense that Andrew was avoiding her. She wasn't sure how to break the ice, until one day, about a month after she had last seen Andrew in the hospital visiting Justin, Justin phoned her about a decision he had made.

After her conversation with Justin, she felt excited and felt that she should tell Andrew, but she hesitated at first, as she didn't want to meddle with their lives. She thought about first asking Adrian's opinion, but then she dialled the number. 'Maybe there is a chance for those two, after all?'

Her heart was pounding as the phone rang, and luckily Andrew picked up right away. "Hi, Andrew, how are you?"

"Thanks, I'm fine. Everything okay with you?" Andrew tried not to sound awkward.

"I have something to tell you that I thought you should know."

"What's the matter?" A thought came into his mind, 'Is she pregnant?'

"Listen, Justin called off the engagement with Rebecca last week and she went back to the USA alone a few days ago." Andrew's mind went blank and he almost dropped his phone. He was stunned by the news. "Are you still there?" Olivia was wondering if Andrew was still listening.

"What happened?" Andrew was really surprised.

"They came by one night before Rebecca returned back to the USA. Apparently, they had a long and honest discussion. They both agreed they wouldn't go ahead with the wedding and they called off the engagement. They agreed to part as friends, but I could tell Rebecca was upset."

Andrew was quiet, as he didn't know what to say. He hadn't heard from Justin since the last time he'd seen him in hospital, so it came as a shock to him that Justin had broken off the engagement. Though he missed him and thought of Justin with every beat of his heart, but even if they met up again, he didn't know what they would say to each other.

"Andrew, are you okay?" Olivia asked nervously, as Andrew went quiet again.

Andrew stood up and walked around the living room. He couldn't sit still. "Thanks for letting me know. So, how are you doing? Any news about your plans for IVF treatments?" Purposely, Andrew changed the subject.

"We are still talking and discussing it with our GP and will find a decision soon."

"Listen, thanks for calling. I might come to Glasgow one evening next week and we can catch up." Andrew felt he needed time alone to digest and process what he had just learned about Justin. 'Why did Olivia tell me this? Did Justin want me to know?' After Andrew ended the phone call with Olivia, he sat on the bar stool in the kitchen for a while with lots of questions in his mind and a mixture of feelings and emotions.

Although he hadn't smoked for years, he had a sudden urge for cigarettes. He looked outside the window, it was dark, windy and was pouring down with heavy rain. Andrew hesitated for a bit, but still put on a raincoat and went to the nearest convenience store. 'Maybe some rain and fresh air can clear my head.' He desperately needed something to distract himself.

As he opened the front entrance of his building, he thought, 'for the love of God, this had better be worth it. I am losing my mind getting cigarettes this late and in this weather.'

After he got home, he quickly dried himself, lit a cigarette and made himself a cup of herbal tea. He sat on the sofa in the living room and took a drag, and even without inhaling it he coughed heavily, he had never got used to the sensation and strong taste of smoking.

After he calmed down, he acted from his heart and not from his brain. He texted Justin:

Hi, Justin, hope you are well. Just wondering about your recovery. Andrew.

He put down the phone and stared at it for a few minutes; then he watched TV for a while before going to bed. He was hoping for a reply from Justin, but at the same time he was afraid his reply might bring back some uncomfortable feelings.

He got up the next morning and was working as usual, but checked his phone from time to time, although his phone would have automatically alerted him with a sound for any incoming text messages. By eleven a.m., a text reply from Justin came in:

Hi, I am getting better. How are you? How was your trip to Hong Kong? Must have been an exciting trip? Justin.

Nice hearing from you. Glad to know you are getting better. Andrew.

Justin replied right away.

I am leaving Glasgow next month and going back to the USA, as my exchange programme is coming to an end. Due to my accident, I am allowed to submit my final paper from home.

Andrew hesitated at first, but then texted:

Would you like to come for dinner one evening? What about Friday?

Andrew answered a few emails and spoke to a new potential customer, and when he looked at his phone, he saw a message from Justin.

Great! Looking forward to your cooking. Justin.

Andrew contemplated whether or not to invite Justin to stay over, but decided not to, as he didn't want to give the wrong impression of the dinner invitation.

Andrew was excited at first about seeing Justin again, but then he was wondering about the call from Olivia. 'How come Justin didn't mention in his text about the break-up with Rebecca? Does he know that Olivia told me?'

Andrew tried to keep himself busy for the next few days. As he started to tidy up on Friday morning, he started to doubt whether it had been a good idea to meet up with Justin, as he didn't want to get hurt again.

Around midday, he received a message from Justin. Before reading it, Andrew initially thought Justin had texted to cancel. 'I will be a bit disappointed, but then it will come as a relief as well.' Andrew then read the message:

Hi, I will take the bus to reach Edinburgh and should be at your place around five-thirty p.m. Justin

Andrew felt almost as if they were back to the non-complicated time when they started seeing each other, but he was still cautious with his reply:

Great. See you then. Andrew.

Andrew wasn't working that afternoon, so he had ample time to prepare dinner. He decided to serve the food in the kitchen rather than in the dining room, as it felt less intimate, but he still decorated the breakfast bar area with candles and flowers.

For the first time, he tried making an upside-down cake for dessert and was very pleased with it. As he was admiring his own creation and his thoughts were miles away, he was startled when the phone rang. The call was from Jimi. "Hi, Jimi. Are you back from your holiday?"

"Yes, I've been back for two days. Just called and spoke to my mum. So grateful for all you have done for her. I'm so worried about her." Jimi sounded very concerned.

"Jimi, the test she took showed no trace of blood, which was a good thing. Her GP just wanted to be sure and referred her for other tests. Besides, we need to find out why she has those symptoms. Don't worry, I am here." Andrew tried to lighten the conversation.

"I'm coming to Edinburgh on Monday for a week. I want to spend some time with her. Can I stay with you?"

"Why do you even need to ask? Of course. Send me your arrival time and I'll pick you up from the airport." Andrew wanted to tell Jimi about Justin's visit later that evening, but decided not to at the last minute.

"I know how to get to your place. I'll just take a taxi. It's not like I've never been there before. We really enjoyed our trip touring Asia. I'll tell you more when I see you next week. Wait, Vincent wants to say hello."

"Hi, Andrew. Hope everything is okay with you. We had such a good time in Asia. When are you coming to visit us in Spain?"

"Hi, Vincent, great you had a good holiday." Andrew looked at his watch and saw that it was now four-thirty p.m. He still had dinner to prepare.

"Listen, I will discuss it with Jimi when he comes next week and book the ticket then. Thanks for the invitation."

"Great. Bye-bye. Jimi's here." Vincent handed the phone back to Jimi.

"See you next week. Once again, thank you." Jimi's voice almost cracked.

"See you next week, and I will give you a full report on all the details and the additional tests she needs to take."

Andrew managed to take a shower before making the last preparations for dinner. Just after five-thirty p.m., the intercom buzzer rang. He pressed the button. His heart was beating so fast he could almost hear it. He opened the door and saw Justin coming out of the lift. As Justin walked towards Andrew, he noticed that he had a slight but visible limp and that one of his hands was still in plaster.

They greeted each other awkwardly as they tried to put their arms around each other for a hug, but failed. They avoided eye contact with each other.

"Come in. Wow, your arm is still in plaster?"

"Yes. I'll tell you more about it." Justin handed Andrew a shopping bag containing a bottle of red wine.

"Thanks. Come in. We will eat in the kitchen today. Hope that's okay?" Andrew took the bottle from

Justin's hand and made a welcome gesture with his arm.

"Great. Actually, it's better to sit on a taller bar stool. I don't need to bend my leg too much. It still hurts." Justin walked into the kitchen.

Andrew poured red wine into two glasses and handed Justin a glass.

"My arm is healing right now, but once I am back in the US, they will have to operate on it again to insert a metal screw." Justin pointed to the place where the metal screw would be inserted.

"Good God. That must have been a bad accident you had."

"I'm okay. It will just take time. It just looked worse than the reality, and I will be okay soon." Justin smiled.

They became more relaxed as the evening progressed. They were like they were when they first spent time together. Justin confirmed that he was leaving in a month's time, as his studies requirement in Edinburgh would end. Justin was fascinated when Andrew told him his plans for expanding his business.

"I was approached by a business associate to buy and manage a care home. I need time to consider it, but I think it is an interesting business investment." Andrew's eyes sparkled.

"I am so impressed with what you have achieved." Justin suddenly stood up, slowly walked towards Andrew with his limping foot and gave him a hug.

Andrew froze, not knowing how to react or what to say. He slightly pushed Justin away. "Do you want some dessert? I made an upside-down cake for the first time and it hasn't turned out too badly." Andrew tried to ease the awkwardness as he saw Justin go back to his seat, slightly embarrassed and red-faced.

"Oh, thanks. I would like to try a piece. But only a small piece. I know how your servings are," Justin teased.

"Come on, you're still growing. You can handle it." Andrew sliced the cake and served Justin a large piece.

"Don't tell me you're not eating. Oh, this is good." Justin made a sound to indicate his appreciation of the cake.

"I will later. Do you want something else to drink? Coke or juice?" Andrew saw that Justin had hardly touched his wine.

"I am fine for the moment. Thanks. May I use the bathroom?"

"Of course, you know where it is." Andrew stood up to make room for Justin to pass.

While Justin was in the bathroom, Andrew waited in the kitchen; with the dim lights and candles, his mind wandered to different places. He wasn't sure whether it was a good idea to offer Justin to stay over. 'Strange he never mentioned Rebecca and the break-up of their engagement.' That was his last thought before he heard Justin coming back to the kitchen.

He was still standing when Justin walked in the kitchen and suddenly Justin put his one arm around Andrew. Andrew's body tensed.

"Don't you want to hug me?" Justin whispered in Andrew's ear.

'Don't tempt me. I can't go there again.'

"Just one hug," Justin softly said in Andrew's ear.

Andrew resisted and hesitated for a good while, and then he melted. He put his arms around Justin and gently stroked Justin's back. "Do you want to stay over?" The words came out of Andrew's mouth without him even thinking about it. Justin straightened up and used his one hand to slightly push Andrew away.

"I must go now. I will take the next bus back to Glasgow." Suddenly Justin's tone became quite cold and distant.

Andrew stood there feeling like a fool, as he didn't understand what had just happened.

"It's not even eight. Don't you want to stay for a bit?" Andrew hated himself for sounding like he was begging.

"No, thanks. I need to wake up early tomorrow for an appointment for schoolwork, so I want to have an early night." Justin walked towards the door.

"Okay." Andrew sounded defeated. In his head, he was really confused and frustrated.

"Thank you for dinner. It was great seeing you. Maybe I will see you again before I go back to the States." Justin waved to Andrew as he walked to the lift.

The lift doors closed. Andrew stood there, staring at them for some time; then he shut the door.

'What just happened?' Andrew pondered and then became very angry with himself and with Justin. 'I can't believe what just happened.'

He went back to the kitchen and started cleaning up and putting dishes in the dishwasher, but his mind was filled with embarrassment and disappointment, mostly at himself. 'What was I thinking?'

Around ten p.m., he took a shower and made himself a cup of green tea. He sat in his bed, but wasn't ready to go to sleep. He felt that he needed to know what just happened. He texted Justin:

Hi, Justin, hope you got home all right. What happened? I am confused. Andrew

Justin texted back right away.

I found it strange that, although you knew, you never mentioned that I called off the engagement with Rebecca. Just because you are persistent, it does not mean it will happen again between us. I am not sure about your intention in wanting to see me. Justin

Andrew felt his blood boil.

I didn't mention about the break off of your engagement because I didn't know if you were comfortable talking about it. Why didn't you bring it up? I am not sure why it became complicated. Andrew

Justin didn't wait long to reply.

Okay. Sorry, maybe I misjudged you and your intentions. I thought maybe you hoped something would happen between us again just because I'm no longer engaged. I am not blaming you for anything. I want people to be honest. I don't like feeling being tricked. Justin

Andrew paused and collected his thoughts before he replied:

I don't understand why you hugged me and insisted that I hug you back? I am confused. Andrew

Another message came from Justin:

It was stupid of me. I was playing with your emotions. I'm sorry. But, you are a successful businessman, and I am still not finished my studies. Not sure what common grounds we share. But my door is always open. Justin

Andrew looked at the last message and then back through all the messages again and felt an overwhelming sense of stupidity and disappointment. He so wanted to reply back, but refrained himself from doing so because he had lost some of his respect for Justin and wasn't sure that there was any point in reasoning with him.

Sill, something in Justin's text got Andrew thinking. 'Maybe Justin made a good point. I am approaching fifty, and what am I doing with someone who is thirty? Were my intentions so innocent? Was it so wrong for me to like him? If he didn't feel comfortable being with me, why did we spend so much time together? Why did he even come tonight?' Many thoughts and questions were in his mind.

Although he laid in the dark in his bed, he felt his face turn red and his heart fill with sorrow and even a bit of shame. He was angry that he had made himself vulnerable and felt let down, as he had opened his heart to Justin again.

Suddenly, the phone rang and Sami's caller ID appeared.

Andrew alarmed. 'Why is she calling at this hour?'

He answered quickly. "Andrew, hope I have not woken you up. I wasn't able to sleep, so I called and spoke to my mother and then to Jimi. Many thanks for helping my mother." Sami was weeping.

"Sami, no need to thank me. It's nothing. Jimi is coming over next week and we will both go with your mother to the hospital for other tests. Her GP doesn't believe she has bowel cancer, but just to be sure he has referred her for other tests to be taken. How are you doing? How is your pregnancy?" Andrew felt good hearing from Sami. Her voice cheered him up.

"I am doing well. Thanks. I spoke to my husband and Jimi and I have decided to travel to Edinburgh next month and stay there till after the baby is born." Sami sounded excited.

"Wow, I'm very happy for you. If there's no room at your mother's place, as Joey is there as well, you can always stay at my place, in Nathan's old room." For the first time, Andrew wasn't sad talking about Nathan.

"Thanks for the offer. I will let you know once I have my travel date confirmed." Sami was emotional again.

"Sami, don't be sad. We will all be here for your mother. She is a strong woman. She told me she is not ready to go just yet, as she will be a grandmother again." Andrew tried to lift Sami's spirits.

"Thanks. After the baby is born, I hope I can persuade my mother to come back to Hong Kong and stay with us for a longer period so she can be part of the baby's life. Oh, I'd better let you go to bed now. It is late for you."

After they hung up, Andrew stared at the phone for a few moments, digesting the whole day and the new chapters and changes ahead.

He closed his eyes and after a while a voice inside him began telling him what and who was important in his life. He felt a sudden sense of clarity. He opened his eyes and reached for his phone. Without hesitation, he deleted the text messages from Justin; then he deleted Justin's phone number and his Messenger account.

Andrew was tired and exhausted, but he had unsettling thoughts running through his mind and he knew he wouldn't be able to go to sleep with all the emotion resulting from what had happened during the day.

'I need to keep myself busy.' Andrew went up to the attic and brought down all the boxes of clothing and things that had belonged to Nathan that he had saved and kept for so many years. Some of them were already in Nathan's old room, some of them he had gathered when clearing up his mother's place and some he had brought home from the USA when he was over there arranging the funeral and bringing back his ashes.

It was eleven years ago that Nathan had died in a car accident, just one month after he turned nineteen. Since then, there hadn't been a single day that Andrew hadn't thought of Nathan, even if only for a few seconds. He'd see something that reminded him of Nathan, his favourite ice cream, food dishes, shops, artists, movies, actors, songs, parts of Edinburgh, colognes, TV shows from his childhood. Actually, at one point everything reminded him of Nathan. But somehow he knew it was time to let go, and he also knew inside it was a learning process he would have to go through to be free from holding on to the past.

Andrew started sorting out Nathan's clothes, putting them in bags to donate to charity shops. He then went through photos, report cards and toys. Each item brought back memories. As he held them close to him, he felt a sense of warmth and closeness to his son. He looked at a photo of his mother bathing baby Nathan. His heart ached, but was filled with love, and tears ran down his face.

He turned off the light. He wrapped himself in a blanket and lay in the bed in Nathan's old room. Although the room had turned into a guest room, in his heart Andrew always referred to it as Nathan's old room.

He was suddenly hit by an overwhelming fatigue. 'I will see you tomorrow.' Andrew closed his eyes, and he was finally able to fall asleep.

Chapter 20
Letting Go

The next morning, when Andrew woke up, it was a cloudy day, but he didn't care and he didn't take along an umbrella. He went out and took the bus. It was cold, though he didn't realise it. He ran when he got off the bus just outside of the graveyard gate.

As Andrew was reaching Nathan's grave, he lost his balance. He held on tightly to Nathan's tombstone in order not to fall over.

Standing in front of Nathan's grave, Andrew was puzzled at his own feeling of shame and guilt for being emotionally involved with Justin. He began to sob uncontrollably and for the first time he was able to release his emotions.

He wept over Nathan's death. He wept over his father, who had left him and his mother as he was growing up. He wept over not being a better son to his mother. At the same time, he also felt guilty for not taking more chances in life and not being happier.

Everything for him was just jogging along okay. From the outside it looked as if he had done quite well, living a comfortable life. But nobody understood how he struggled with the loss of his beloved son; such a cruel and harsh reality he would have to live with for the rest of his life.

'Have I failed my life? Where do I go from here?' he asked himself.

Andrew looked round and gradually noticed that the rain had stopped. At first, he hadn't even realised it had been raining. He was soaking wet.

He felt, at that exact moment, as if the rain had washed away his guilt and he'd been unburdened from all the grief and sorrow that he'd carried for most of his life. Suddenly, when he looked up and he saw a hint of sunshine cutting through the clouds, there it was, an extraordinary rainbow.

He stared at the sky for a while and imagined capturing the rainbow as it faded. His thoughts then recalled a session he had had with a counsellor a few years before.

Several months after coming back from the USA after Nathan's death, his GP had referred him to a professional for a few counselling sessions. In the beginning, it was difficult for Andrew to share his feelings and emotional thoughts about Nathan's death, especially with this new person.

'What a waste of time!' Many times, Andrew wanted to quit the sessions. But somehow he continued, and it took a few visits before he was slowly able to open up. He was finally able to share with the counsellor his anger and frustration over having to bury his own son. At the same time, he talked about how he felt responsible for his mother's sorrow about Nathan's death and him not in a relationship. At one point he also told the counsellor that for a long time he had had this image of a little boy recurrently appearing in his dreams.

"Although the image came to me faceless, I felt strongly connected to this little boy and felt that I wanted and needed to protect and comfort him." Andrew was puzzled with his own recounting of the dreams. The counsellor didn't say anything, but looked tenderly and supportively at Andrew.

"Does it mean I am considering having another child, or is this boy Nathan? But how could that boy be Nathan, as the image had been recurring for as long as he could remember, even before Nathan was born." Andrew was surprised by his own thoughts and felt a bit guilty about imagining having another child, as if it was almost betraying Nathan.

No one said a word for a while. Then the counsellor broke the silence and asked, "Who do you think this child represents? Have you ever considered the little boy could be your inner child? It is you whom you want to love, protect and comfort?"

Andrew was stunned. He looked at the counsellor then stared at the ceiling and thought to himself, 'How is that possible? What does that even mean, my inner child?' He contemplated this for a long while. The room was so quiet; both he and the counsellor didn't say anything to each other. One could almost hear a pin drop.

Eventually, Andrew broke down in tears, as he came to realise the image of the little boy was himself. He was also able to see clearly that he was never able to connect emotionally with himself or be mindful of his own feelings, it was beyond his imagination that it was possible that the image of the little boy could subconsciously represent his need for love, self-forgiveness and to be able to let go of grief and pain.

Suddenly Andrew was brought back to reality, catching sight of a squirrel effortlessly climbing down from a tree and then running across the graveyard to jump up into another. He admired it with fascination.

He then thought about Justin and admitted to himself he would be lying if he thought he could completely erase Justin from his mind and heart right away; but Andrew knew for his own good he had to let Justin go. 'It is not possible to just turn on and off strong feelings for someone. But Justin has his own destiny to follow and will have to go through it, making his own mistakes like everyone else. Whatever happens, it's no longer my concern and probably it never was,' Andrew thought. By fate, their paths had crossed again and they had parted by choice. At that moment Andrew felt his blood boil with sense of intense irritation. He experienced overwhelming sadness and disappointment when he came to the realisation that he had suppressed all his emotions his entire life, depriving himself of truly expressing his own anger, his sorrows and even joy. He had an overwhelming urge to shout out, as he felt he owed himself so much expression he had choked down for so long.

Eventually, his turmoil released and he calmed down. Andrew then thought about Sami and her baby, which would change his life. 'Yes, there must be an ending, but there are also new beginnings. I need to turn the page and find new chapters and challenges to fulfil me.' He made a promise to himself. He closed his eyes, as everything around him became quiet. Time just stood still. Thoughts seeped in. He whispered:

'One day.

One moment.

One breath.

One heartbeat.

One smile.

One possibility.

And one hope.'

Feeling somewhat enlightened, Andrew opened his eyes. He took a deep breath and exhaled slowly, with the hope that one day, sooner or later, he would be reunited with Nathan and his mother, and finally the unity of the three of them will again be complete. He looked down at Nathan's grave and then looked around and up, and he noticed birds twittering, cars and buses driving by outside the gate of the graveyard, and he even heard the sound of the wind howling. 'I am alive.' He had a smile on his face.

'I am so fortunate to have had my mum and Nathan in my life. They are with me in every breath I take. What is important for me now is Mama Evelyn's health and Sami's baby. I will be there for them, as they have been for me. They are the people who are worthy of my love.' In that moment he felt enlightenment, at peace with himself. 'Letting go. Letting go.' He found a sense of self-acceptance, ready to come out of his own shell. Significantly, for the first time in his life he felt he had the strength to lift the huge burden of self-inflicted pain and self-blame and let it go.